Ultimate Sacrifice

Men of Courage Book One

K.C. LYNN

Dedication

This book is dedicated to my beautiful friend Anna.

You are one of my best friends in this book world and I value your friendship.

Thank you for always being there. Austin and Zoey are for you.

PROLOGUE

My hand shakes from the intense precision I require, sweat dotting my forehead as each wire is carefully constructed and wrapped.

It's been so long since I've given in to this urge; I'd forgotten what it feels like. The power that accompanies the thrill, but this time, it's about more than power.

It's about revenge.

Soon there will be nothing left of this town but ash, and everyone in it will feel the wrath of my vengeance.

CHAPTER ONE

Zoey

Anticipation slides down my spine, my pulse racing at a rapid pace as we drive down a long gravel road just outside of town, my heart and body fully aware of the man next to me.

I've waited a long time for this night. A night I am going to allow myself to have just this once then I'll hold the beautiful memories close to me when it's all over.

My gaze shifts to Austin, admiring his strong profile and the hard angle of his jaw, the glow from the dashboard illuminating his handsome face. One I often admire from afar when he and his friends come into the bar for a drink. Whether it's after a long day of fire fighting or a grueling hockey game, they spend many nights socializing at Overtime. Considering I own the place, it's definitely a bonus.

Weeks ago, I hosted a date auction with some of the most eligible bachelors of Colorado, the courageous men of Fire Station Two. It was for a cause that I hold very dear to my heart. All the proceeds were donated to the Children's Miracle Center. A place where my eleven-year-old sister, Chrissy, has resided for the past three years. She has cerebral palsy, one of the most severe cases her doctors have ever seen, which is why she requires assisted living.

The auction was a success, as I knew it would be. We raised a lot of money. The men were less than enthused to be bid on by a bunch of hungry women but they did it for me anyway. They know how important that center is for my sister.

It also gave me the perfect opportunity to snag a date with Austin

Hawke, a man I now consider a friend but feel so much more for. It turned into quite the bidding war between me and two other women but I was not going to back down, which is why I topped the bid at one thousand dollars. I knew it would be money well spent, not only for myself but also for Chrissy. However, when it came time to pay, I found out Austin had already taken care of it. My heart warms at the reminder, a small smile stealing my lips.

Sensing the weight of my stare, Austin spares me a glance. "What's going on in that pretty head of yours, Zoey girl?"

"Zoey girl." A nickname he has given me for as long as I have known him. It makes me smile every time he uses it.

I rest back against my seat, keeping my eyes trained on his handsome face. "Just thinking about how much fun I've had with you today."

It's been a date I'll remember forever. We started the afternoon by going on a long hike through the mountains, a trail Austin visits frequently. The scenery was incredible and my fingers twitched, wishing I had brought my camera with me. Photography is a hobby of mine that I don't get to do often and today I experienced some of the most beautiful sights this world has to offer.

Afterward, we had a picnic that was packed with all my favorite food; lying next to the basket was also a bouquet of daffodils—my favorite flower. Turns out my best friend, Sam, gave Austin a helping hand by sharing the information about me. He put a lot of thought into this date and it has meant more to me than he will ever know.

Conversation flowed well throughout dinner. I was riveted by everything he shared about himself, especially about his life as a firefighter. His career is just one of the many things I've always admired about him. Our meal ended with us watching the sunset. The red, orange, and purple hues danced across the sky, sinking beyond the mountains. It was beautiful and peaceful.

A moment I will treasure forever.

He reaches over the console and takes my hand in his, sending a warm sensation up my arm. "It's not over yet, I'm nowhere near done with you."

My belly dips with anticipation at the underlying promise in his words. To finish the night off he's taking me to the house that he's been building for the past year, seated just on the outskirts of town. I'm both excited and anxious of the prospect for how the night will end.

Unlike me, Austin doesn't look the least bit nervous; his large, fit body is nothing but relaxed behind the wheel.

"And for the record," he says, speaking again. "Next time you want a date, Zoey, an auction isn't necessary, all you have to do is ask." His eyes seek mine in the dark truck, seizing the moment. "You have to know by now that I'd take you anywhere. You just have to give me the chance."

His words are both soothing and heartbreaking. If he only knew how long I've wanted this, how much I wish I could date like a normal twenty-five-year-old. Every date would be shared with him. Unfortunately, that is not the life I've been given. Not with the responsibility of my sister. She needs me too much. Between the bar and taking care of her, there is no time left for my love life.

I'm saved from having to reveal that when he turns off the gravel road, driving up a dirt path that leads to his house. When the log home comes into view, I gasp in awe of its rustic beauty. There's a massive porch that wraps around the entire house. Right away, I envision hanging ferns and a swing big enough to lie on. A place where you can sit and appreciate the beautiful nature that God has so graciously created. Even though the house is unfinished, you can't help but see its potential.

Austin clears his throat, breaking into my admiration. "It's still a work in progress."

"It's beautiful," I whisper, my attention anchored on the sight before me.

Reaching into the backseat, he grabs a lantern and turns it on, bringing the truck to a soft glow. "Come on, I'll show you the inside."

He climbs out and comes around to offer me his hand, helping me down. Once my feet hit the hard dirt, his fingers curl around mine. My heart dances in my chest at the simple gesture as we walk up to the house.

"Be careful, one of the stairs isn't screwed in all the way." He releases my hand and wraps an arm around my waist, lifting me over the stair in question before placing me back on my feet.

I suddenly find myself winded, the side of my body that was just pressed against his blazing from the contact. I've never been affected like this before. This need, this pull, it draws me in and never lets go.

He hands me the lantern as he digs into his pocket for his keys and unlocks the door. Dusty wood creaks beneath my light footsteps as I enter inside. Once again I'm struck by the unique craftsmanship. There's just enough moonlight pouring in from the floor to ceiling windows to offer a generous view of the open concept.

"Let me start a fire," he says, stepping around me.

"That's not something you hear a fireman say every day," I tease.

A low chuckle rumbles from his chest, the sound trickling across my skin with a delicious tingle.

"Do you want a drink?" he asks.

"I'd love one."

"Beer okay?"

"That's great. Thanks."

While he walks over to the far corner where the fireplace is, I lift the lantern and do some more exploring. I check out the three framed bedrooms, making sure to be mindful of all the scattered tools and building materials lying around. Immediately, I know which one will be the master due to its size. Much like the rest of the house, this room is made up of large windows, giving a picturesque view of outside. Amongst the tall trees and mountains, I can hear a small creek, its rushing water adding to the atmosphere.

I can't help but wonder what it would be like to wake up here in the morning. Sun dripping with the day's promise and birds chirping with life.

A dream home if I've ever seen one. Maybe one day I'll have something like this. A place for Chrissy and me to call home that will be wheelchair accessible and able to accommodate all of her needs.

I push aside my fruitless dreams for now and walk out of the room, entering into the half-finished kitchen. My fingers dance along the dusty granite counters that have just been installed. There's a hole in the center where the sink will go.

"Like what you see?"

I spin around on a gasp and find Austin standing right behind me.

An amused grin curves his lips. "Sorry, I didn't mean to scare you."

"It's okay," I tell him, sounding ridiculously breathless. Though, that has more to do with his close proximity than my frantic heartbeat.

He passes me one of the two bottles he holds. I accept it with a smile and place the lantern down next to me.

"So, what do you think?" he asks again, gesturing around us.

"I love it. It's already so beautiful I can only imagine what it will look like when it's completely finished."

"Thanks. I've been working on it for so long it feels good to finally see an end in sight."

"How much longer until you move in?"

"Another few weeks and it will be livable but the finished product is still months away. I have a lot more I want to do."

It amazes me that he has built this with his own two hands. "Do you have much help?"

"Yeah, my dad comes when he can and so do Jake and Cam," he says, talking about his two best friends who also work with him at the fire department. "Of course, they come a lot more when I offer free beer," he finishes with a sexy smirk.

A chuckle escapes me. "Free beer is always a good incentive."

His smile fades, his warm brown eyes pinning me in place. Setting his beer down on the counter, he plants his hands on either side of my body, caging me in. My grip on my bottle tightens, my breath catching at the way he invades my personal space.

"What is it you're wanting here, Zoey?" he asks, cutting right to the chase. "What are you hoping to get out of this?"

It's now or never.

My tongue darts out to wet my dry lips as I steel my nerves. "You." The confession is nothing more than a whisper. "I want you but I only have tonight."

"Why?" he asks, eyes searching mine.

"Because I can't give you any more than that. Between the bar and Chrissy, I don't have time for anything else. I probably shouldn't even be here now," I tell him, guilt bubbling inside of me when I think about my sister all alone at the center. "But I am and I have tonight, if you want me."

My heart bangs inside of my chest, echoing in my ears as he peers back at me.

He dips his face closer, his nose brushing my cheek. "What if I want more than one night? What if I don't want to let you go after this is over?"

My eyes drift closed, disappointment crushing me. I wish I could tell him I want that, too. I'd love nothing more than to spend many nights in his arms but...I can't. I can't be selfish.

"I'm sorry. I can't have more, not when I have Chrissy to look after. I'm all she has."

He rests his forehead against the side of mine but I keep my eyes closed, unable to witness his rejection that I'm sure is to come.

A sharp breath impales my lungs when I feel his warm lips against my cheek, pressing a gentle kiss before moving to my ear. "Then I guess we better make this night count."

My eyes spring open, his handsome face hovering before me. He closes the remaining distance between us, his lips descending, slow and sure, capturing mine in a heated caress. The subtle contact rocks the very foundation of who I am.

The beer bottle slips from my hands, crashing to the floor as my fingers dive into his hair, my need for him racing to the surface and exploding like dynamite.

Growling, he cups my bottom, lifting me off my feet. "You taste so fucking sweet, Zoey girl."

I want to tell him the same thing but I can barely manage a coherent thought at the moment let alone speak it.

My legs lock around his lean waist as he walks us over to the fireplace, his mouth continuing to dominate mine.

My back meets the blanket that's been laid out, Austin's hard body following down on top of me. His erection settles between my legs, nudging the exact spot I crave to feel him most.

A moan shoves from my throat as I reach for the bottom of his shirt, needing to feel his skin upon mine. He rises to his knees and reaches behind his back, pulling the soft material over his head to reveal…perfection.

The glow of the roaring flames dance across his sun-kissed skin, showcasing every hard line of his body. From his broad shoulders and strong chest down to his sculpted abs that look like they've been carved from stone.

Before I have a chance to explore all those hard lines, he moves for my tank top, inching it up my stomach. I lift up just enough for him to clear it over my head. His warm brown eyes darken as they become fixated on my black lace bra. A garment I splurged on just for this night with him.

My teeth sink into my bottom lip as his hand coasts up my stomach, creating a path of heat in its wake. He flicks the front clasp, brushing the lace cups aside to bare me to his stare.

"So fucking pretty." The deep vibration of his voice races through my body. His face dips, lips descending to draw a hard nipple into his mouth.

A heated whimper breaches my lips, my back arching to get closer. His free hand covers my other breast; fingers teasing my aching tip while his teeth torment the other. Every pull of his mouth and fiery lash of his tongue drives my need higher.

I lift my hips, seeking friction for the fierce ache between my legs. "Austin, please."

"Easy, baby," he soothes, trailing his warm, wet mouth down my stomach. "We have all night."

I don't want to wait all night. I already feel like I've been waiting a lifetime for this moment with him. On the loneliest nights it's his face I see and his touch I feel. Now I can say everything I imagined before this pales in comparison to the real thing.

He flicks the button of my shorts and drags them down my legs, taking my lace thong with them. Another growl shreds his throat, his hand snaking between my legs. "This is all for me, isn't it, baby?"

"Yes," I gasp, desire seeping into my blood with heated force.

"We're going to get this pretty pussy nice and ready for me." I barely comprehend the erotic words before he drops down, his tongue delving through my wet center.

My cry of pleasure tears through the room, hips bucking as the most beautiful sensations ravage my body.

"So fucking sweet." His groan ripples through me, adding to the pleasure.

I thrash beneath him, my fingers tangling in his hair as he devours me in a way I've only ever dreamed about. He bands an arm over my hips, holding me in place as his tongue works deeper—harder.

The moment he adds a finger into my entrance, I catapult into another universe. His name pours from my lips as pleasure whips through my senses.

"That's it, Zoey girl. Come all over my face." Austin never falters until he takes every last drop from me. My chest heaves, lungs working hard for air as he climbs back up my body. His lips cherish every inch of skin he passes before he takes my mouth in a searing kiss, igniting another inferno within.

I moan at the lingering taste of myself, the flavor making my senses reel. My hands move to his belt, eager for more.

I'm ready for all of him.

He reaches down to help me, his efforts as urgent as mine. Once he sheathes himself with the condom, he lines himself up, his jaw ticking in restraint. "You ready for me, baby?"

"Yes," I whisper without hesitation.

The tip of him presses inside of me seconds before he pushes forward, filling me with every generous inch of him. An army of sensations implode through my body, settling deep into my heart. I wrap my arms around his shoulders and bury my face in his neck as I become overwhelmed with emotion.

His body stills, a groan rumbling his chest. "Sweet Zoey," he croons, his lips brushing my ear, "we're so good together."

We're better than good. Nothing has ever felt so right, but I've always known we would be. I knew if this night were to ever happen between us we would create magic.

That's why, in this moment, I choose to hold him close. To not let him move and just savor the way his body feels pressed against mine, how he fills me so perfectly, knowing after tonight I will never feel anything like this again.

"How the hell am I supposed to let you go now?" The torment in his voice has pain infiltrating my chest.

I don't have an answer for him. I have no idea how I am going to walk away after this. The thought has emotion inching up my throat but I swallow it back, refusing to let it penetrate this perfect moment.

He presses a kiss to my shoulder, my cheek, then my mouth, his lips going from gentle to commanding in a matter of seconds. My fingers dig into his broad shoulders as he begins moving, slowly at first, each stroke more beautiful than the last as he kisses a part of my soul that's never been touched before.

"I love feeling you inside of me," I admit before I can stop myself.

"It's fucking perfect. *You're* perfect." His mouth parts from mine as he braces himself above me, driving himself harder and deeper.

"Yes!" My leg curls around his back as I completely surrender myself, loving the way his strong body strains beneath my fingertips.

"It's good, baby, isn't it?"

"So good," I moan, the connection between us undeniable.

"That's because it's us, Zoey. You and me, and together we're fucking dynamite." He covers my mouth with his, never faltering his delectable thrusts. If anything, he gives me more, hammering into me harder and more possessively.

Sweat soaks our skin, our bodies melding together the same way our hearts are. My stomach begins to tighten, fingers clawing his shoulders as I feel myself teetering on the edge of precious destruction once again.

"Austin," I whisper against his lips, not wanting this to end, wishing I could stop time.

"Give into it, baby. I'm nowhere near done with you."

It's those words that have me letting go. This orgasm is even more powerful than the last, robbing my heart and stealing what's left of it.

Austin follows not long after me, burying his face in my neck on a long, deep groan. I hold him close through it all, making sure to keep my emotion locked up tight.

Afterward, we lie together in a sweaty tangled mess as we try to catch our breaths. My head lies on his chest, his arm braced along my back to keep me close.

"Are you cold?" he asks, mumbling the question.

"No. As long as you stay right here with me, I'll be warm."

His lips press on the top of my head. "I don't plan on leaving this spot for the rest of the night."

Smiling, I bury my face deeper into his chest, clinging to these few precious hours we have together. Eventually, I drift off only to be awakened a short time later by his hands and mouth on my body.

We make love twice more through the night, each time more perfect than the last. I make sure to commit it all to memory. Every touch and kiss we share I store in a place that will only ever be reserved for him.

When dawn breaks and I'm no longer able to put off the dreadful moment, I slip out from under his arm as quietly as possible and get dressed. I gaze down at his sleeping face, my heart shattering in a million pieces to know I will never see him this way again.

Unable to stop myself, I kneel down next to him, brushing my lips across his one more time. Then I do one of the hardest things I've ever had to do.

I walk away.

No doubt he'll be angry when he wakes up to find me gone but it will be easier this way, for the both of us. Knowing this doesn't make it any less painful though.

Gravel crunches beneath my tennis shoes as I start my long walk home, the fresh air doing very little for my wounded heart.

I can't be angry at the life I've been given. I love my sister and the responsibility of taking care of her has never been a burden. She's the reason I wake up every single day. My reason for everything I do.

But I can't help but wonder, *what if.*

What if things were different and I could keep Austin? What if I could do the one thing I love most and capture the beautiful sights of this world that most of us take for granted. More importantly, what if my sister wasn't disabled and could care for herself? To be able to fall in love with another and have a family of her own one day.

It's that thought that has my tears flowing freely. For the life I wish I could have, but even more, for the life Chrissy has been denied. That's what makes me continue to put one foot in front of the other, leaving behind a night I'll never forget and a man I will long for until the day I die.

CHAPTER TWO

Austin

Two months later

S moke consumes the air, billowing around me. It tries sucking me into its black abyss but I fight through the chaos, refusing to let it swallow me. Despite the fiery destruction, everything inside of me is calm and collected.

Focused.

I can hear every breath of oxygen I pull in from my tank. It echoes in my ears and rushes through my blood. Beads of sweat drip into my eyes and trickle down my face. Most importantly, I feel my brothers close by, fighting the roaring flames next to me.

This is the job. A risk we take. A sacrifice we all make.

We got the call not even fifteen minutes ago about the abandoned warehouse being up in flames. From the outside it looked manageable, but once we entered we were met with a raging beast.

"Talk to me, Hawke. What do you guys have going on in there?" My captain's voice booms through my earpiece.

"We managed to make it to the upper level but the situation has escalated. I've never seen anything like this, Cap. Something doesn't feel right. There's an odor in here I can't place."

"I smell it, too," Jake says, speaking into his mic. He stands to my left, only a few feet away.

"We need a different plan of attack."

"Agreed," Cam adds.

"Screw that," Declan argues. "We got this, guys."

"*Not from in here!*" *My voice is stern, leaving no room for argument.*

Declan is a rookie and eager. I get it, this is what we're trained for, what we wait for, but he is not qualified for something of this magnitude. None of us are with the plan we have in place now.

"All right. All of you, out," *Cap orders. "We'll cover it from the outside until more reinforcements show up."*

"Copy," *Cam says from my right. "I'm backing out now."*

Jake withdraws next.

"Declan?" *I call, waiting for his check-in behind me.*

"Yeah, yeah," *he grumbles.*

The moment I feel the tug of the hose with his descent, I retreat, my eyes never straying from the raging beauty before me. How something can be so beautiful yet destructive at the same time is a complete mind fuck but it's one of the reasons I love what I do.

"Hold up, there's a cracked door open over here," *Declan bellows. "It looks clean, maybe we can approach it from here."*

I spin around, barely making out his shadow as he moves left, reaching for the door. "Do not enter! It's not secure."

My order comes too late. Dread grips my chest in a fit of rage as flames escape, roaring with suffocating heat and engulfing Declan in the blink of an eye.

The blast is furious, knocking me off my feet. Pain radiates through my whole body, sucking the air out of my lungs, but nothing hurts as much as the grief spearing my chest like a hot iron poker, the knowledge that I just watched Declan turn to ash right before my eyes.

I come awake on a roar, a cold sweat covering my skin as I shoot upright. My lungs expand painfully, trying to take in air as I fight to even my breathing. I glance at the clock and realize my alarm is blaring. Hitting the silence button, I grab my cell that lies next to it and find a text from Cam.

I'll pick you up at ten. Cap wants us at the church early.

My gut knots, my mind and heart not ready for this. To say the final goodbye to a fellow brother. One I was supposed to watch over and protect.

With that tormenting thought in mind, I climb to my feet and head for the shower, hoping to wash away the guilt and despair that has been suffocating me for the past week.

The day passes in a sea of blue but the pain is transparent, written on the faces of everyone here, including my fellow brothers. Being a pallbearer has to be one of the hardest things I've ever done. It's supposed to be an honor yet I feel undeserving.

I'm not the only one who feels it. All of us do. Cam, Jake, and I have been best friends since we were kids, playing hockey together our entire lives and now we fight fires side by side, always watching out for one another. When one of us bleeds, we all bleed, and right now is no different.

As hard as this has been on us, I think Cap is taking it the worst. In his thirty-five years, Captain Gyepesi, or whom we like to call Captain Gypsy, has never lost a man on his watch...until now.

The day only gets grimmer when we walk out to the cemetery for the final goodbye and watch as his casket is lowered into the ground. By the time we head back to the parking lot, I'm struggling to breathe through the tightness in my chest.

"I need to get the fuck out of here," Jake says, his voice solemn and body wound tight. "I need a drink."

No one likes a funeral but especially Jake. Not since he had to lay both his parents to rest years ago after a house fire took their lives. It left him to drop his football scholarship to raise his younger sister on his own.

Cam nudges my shoulder and nods across the way. My head turns to see Chief Ramsey striding toward us, grief smothering the older man's face.

Ramsey is the fire chief of the entire division. He's also Declan's uncle and the man who raised him. Their relationship was as strong as father and son. I honestly believe the only reason Declan joined the department was to make Ramsey proud. If that's not a swift kick in the balls for the chief, he also lost his wife a year ago to cancer. As far as I know, Declan was the only family he had left.

Witnessing the sorrow in the other man's eyes only serves to drive that ever-present guilt deeper into my gut.

"Boys," he greets us, shaking each one of our hands, "thanks for being here, Declan had great respect for all of you."

"It was an honor working with him, Sir," Cam replies, speaking for all of us.

Tension fills the air when Chief directs his attention over to Captain.

"Gyepesi." He acknowledges him with a tight nod.

"Ramsey."

There has always been tension between the two of them, something that Cap brushes off anytime we ask. Ramsey, Cap, and Jake's father were all firefighters together, the best of friends until one day they weren't. There's a story there, one none of us know. Not even Declan knew.

"I'm sorry for your loss," Cap continues, filling the silence. "Declan was a good kid and a hell of a firefighter. It was an honor to have him as part of my team, and I have no doubt he would have amounted to great things."

Chief Ramsey shrugs easily but there is no denying the devastation masking his face. "I guess we'll never know now, will we? Looks like you made another bad call, *Cap*."

Cam, Jake, and I share a look, wondering what the hell he means by that. An undeniable pain flashes in the captain's eyes.

The dig against him is unfair; if anyone is to blame it's me, not him. Before I have a chance to speak that, the chief walks away, leaving us in gloomy silence.

"Forget what he said," Cam says, clapping him on the shoulder.

"Wanna come drown your sorrows with us?"

He waves us away. "Nah, you boys go on. I'm going to head back to the station and do some paperwork."

"You sure?" Jake asks.

"Yeah. Behave. I'll see you next shift." After shaking each of our hands, he heads for his truck.

"What do you think Ramsey meant about that call?" Jake asks.

I shrug, having no idea, but I'd be lying if I said I wasn't even more curious now about this tension between them.

Cam, on the other hand, doesn't give it much thought. "Come on, let's get out of here. Overtime?" he asks, looking directly at me.

Two months ago, this would have never been a question, but now it is. All because the girl who owns it has me by the balls and everyone knows it, including me.

The last thing I want right now is to be reminded of everything I want but can't have. Yet, at the same time, I know seeing those baby blues will no doubt help mask the despair and helplessness that has been gripping me for the past week.

"Yeah, let's go."

CHAPTER THREE

Zoey

Every move I make within the bar, I can feel his intense gaze on me. Piercing and penetrating, infiltrating every nerve ending in my body.

Unable to stop myself, I glance over my shoulder. Our eyes collide, his warm brown irises calling to every part of me. There's a sadness in them, a defeat that tugs at my yearning heart.

Austin, Jake, and Cam came in hours ago and have been drinking their pain away for most of the day. A pain they've had to face by saying goodbye to Declan. My heart broke when I heard the news last week, knowing Austin and the others had to be devastated.

I desperately wanted to reach out to him but didn't think my condolences would be welcomed. Ever since I slipped out on him, our friendship has been strained, to say the least. He was as mad as I knew he would be when he woke up that morning to find me gone. It's been hard, really hard. I miss him, but most of all I miss our friendship.

"Hey, hot stuff!"

My eyes dart to Garth Cornell, another patron who has been in here drinking with some coworkers.

"Bring us another round," he demands rudely.

The arrogance pouring off him makes my teeth grind. The four of them come in on the last Friday of every month. They share a few drinks and usually act like pretentious jerks. I put up with it because they spend a lot of money and always tip well. Since things are tight right now, I'll take what I can get.

"You want me to deal with them?" Tara asks, one of the only few waitresses I have on staff. She is not only a great employee but has also become a friend. Something I've missed since my best friend, Sam, moved away.

I shake my head and flash her an appreciative smile. "I got them but thanks."

I make my way behind the counter and set out four tumblers, adding ice to each glass before filling them half full with the best scotch I have. Their tastes are as expensive as their Armani suits.

Frank, my new bartender, comes up behind me and reaches over my shoulder for a glass. "I don't know why you put up with those assholes," he says, gesturing to Garth's table.

I shrug. "Their money is as good as anyone else's, besides, they're harmless."

Most of the time.

He grunts. "Whatever you say, sweetheart. It's your bar."

I smile back at the older man. Decked out in black leather and covered with tattoos, the veteran might have a tough exterior but he's a kind soul. I hired him because I needed the help and figured it's good to have a man around, especially for those late nights when closing. Something Austin used to give me hell about all the time, but I never minded because then he would come in and wait until I finished, making sure I made it to my car safely.

The reminder has my heavy heart swelling in my chest. Shoving the thought aside, I put the four glasses on a tray and carry them over to the waiting table. When I place the last drink down in front of Garth, his hand moves to the inside of my leg, fingers grazing.

I step back and fake the best smile I can manage. "Anything else?"

"Yeah, why don't you pull up a chair and have a drink with us."

We go through this every time he comes in here and my answer is always the same, just like when he asks me out.

"You know I can't do that. I have a bar full of customers."

"It's not that busy. Sit down, Zoey, and have a drink."

Annoyed, I ignore his cocky demand and don't bother repeating myself. "I'll be back to check on you."

I turn away only to have him snag my wrist, his fingers bruising.

Spinning around, my eyes narrow, meeting his dead-on. "If you ever want to come in here again, I suggest you let me go right now."

"Quit being so stubborn and have one drink with us."

He tries tugging me closer but I dig my heels in. "I mean it, Garth. Let go!"

He vanishes before my eyes in a blur of movement. Glass shatters on the floor as the table flips over on its side in a turn of destruction. By the time I register what's happening, Austin has Garth by the throat, pinning him against the wall.

"What part did you not understand?"

A couple of Garth's coworkers move for Austin until Jake and Cam step in front of them.

"That's enough!" I hop over the broken glass and insert myself between the two, facing Austin. My shaky hand presses against his chest. "Let him go."

His furious eyes never stray from Garth, jaw locked tight.

"I'd listen to her," Garth wheezes out. The threat in his voice is as pathetic as he is but I know he has the means to back it up. He could cause Austin a lot of grief if he wanted to.

The thought leaves my stomach in knots. "Please, Austin," I plead, my voice barely above a whisper.

His eyes finally drop to mine, acknowledging me for only a second, but it's a powerful one before he shifts his attention back to Garth. "Put your hands on her again and I'll fucking kill you."

His warning rings through the air with promise. He steps back but not before giving Garth one final shove. I follow him forward as he retreats then turn and face Garth. He massages his throat, his face beginning to lose the purple tinge.

"You aren't welcome here anymore," I tell him. "It's time for you all to leave."

He straightens, his expression hard as granite. He does not like rejection nor does he like his ego to take a beating, which is exactly what Austin just accomplished.

"There are far better places to drink than this dump anyway." His foot meets one of the tipped over chairs, kicking it across the room. He passes by me, way too close for comfort, and the word *bitch* falls from his mouth in a mumble but it's not quiet enough.

It puts Austin in motion but I manage to hold him back, my hand pressing on his strong chest once again. "He's not worth it."

Frank follows them out the door, making sure they leave the premises. Afterward, I blow out a shaky breath, taking in the mess of shattered glass and broken table.

"You all right, Zoey?" Cam asks.

I nod. "Yeah. Thanks." My attention returns to Austin to thank him too but the words die in my throat when I see blood soaking his hand and dripping onto the floor. "You're bleeding!"

He looks down at his wound, flexing his fingers. "It's fine."

It's not "fine" and the pool of blood starting at his feet proves it. I grab the small white towel tucked in my apron and wrap it around his hand. "Come on, I have a first aid kit in the back."

Cam, Jake, and Tara begin cleaning up the mess as I walk Austin into the kitchen, the door swinging closed behind us.

"Sit," I order, pointing to a stool at the stainless steel island.

He complies while I grab the first aid kit, his eyes tracking my every move again. I feel it along my skin, dancing its way into my traitorous heart.

My gaze avoids his as I come to stand in front of him, pulling out what I need to clean and dress his injury. "Let me see," I whisper, unwrapping the bloody towel from his hand.

There's a large gash on his palm and several small cuts on his knuckles. Probably from knocking the glass out of Garth's hand and shattering it.

My fingers tremble as I rip open the gauze and begin cleaning the small wounds; all the while I still feel his eyes on me.

The silence makes me nervous. "Thank you for stepping in and helping me," I say gently. "It wasn't necessary but I appreciate it."

"I don't like anyone touching you."

The possessiveness in his tone has my eyes finally pulling to his. There's so many emotions staring back at me, all the ones I've been harboring since our night together. One stands out amongst the others though—sadness, the day's event clearly weighing heavily on him.

"I'm so sorry about Declan."

My words deepen the pain in his eyes. He lets go of a heavy breath, dropping his forehead on my stomach. "It's my fault," he murmurs, guilt hanging in his voice.

I lift my hand, sifting my fingers through his hair to offer comfort. "Don't say that."

"It is. As his lieutenant it was my job to watch out for him. I told him not to enter but..." He trails off, unable to finish the sentence.

"I don't have all the details but I'm sure Declan wouldn't want you blaming yourself. You're a good man, Austin. The best I've ever known." I rub my hand up and down his back soothingly as he remains silent. "The service was really beautiful."

His head lifts, shock registering on his face. "You were there?"

I nod.

"Why didn't you come talk to me?"

I shrug. "I didn't want to upset you further so I thought it would be best to stay in the back."

"Why do you think it would have upset me?"

All these questions are steering the conversation in a direction I don't want it to go but it's time we have this discussion. It's long overdue. "Because you're angry with me."

"Damn right I'm angry," he says, hardening his tone. "You ran off on me in the middle of the fucking night and walked home on a deserted dirt road all alone."

"I thought it would be easier that way."

"Easier for who?"

I remain silent because we both know the answer. Maybe it makes me a coward but I couldn't bring myself to say goodbye to him, walking away was hard enough. If I had to do it looking into those magnetic eyes, I don't think I would have been able to.

His good hand moves to the side of my face, fingers grazing as he cups my cheek. "Zoey girl, look at me."

I do as he says, tears burning the back of my eyes as I become locked in a gaze of longing with him.

His head dips, perfect lips moving for mine. My heart yearns for it, craves his kiss, but at the last second I turn my face, fighting the war within my heart.

"I'm sorry," I choke out.

His forehead rests on my temple, jaw clenching in frustration. "I know you want this as much as I do. Why are you fighting it so much?"

"It's not about what I want."

"The hell it isn't!"

I flinch at the anger in his voice. "Please try to understand."

"Understand what, Zoey?" he asks, releasing the side of my face.

It leaves me feeling cold and disconnected.

"You don't tell me anything. You don't let me in, so how the hell am I supposed to understand?"

How do I explain it to him? How do I get him to understand that I'm the only person my sister has? To make him understand how horribly she suffers, that she needs all the spare time I have.

"Talk to me," he pleads, his voice softer.

I peer back at him, wanting to confide, to cry on his shoulder and tell him how tired I am. How much I love my sister but her condition takes a toll on me. The horrible thought brings guilt rushing to the surface, slapping me in the face like a cold wet rag. I have no right to feel this way, just like I have no right to lay this burden on him.

"It's complicated," I tell him.

The disappointment in his eyes crushes my soul into tiny fragments.

"Fine. Have it your way." He pushes from the island, climbing to his feet.

"Austin, please," I beg, voice clogged with my barely contained emotions.

He doesn't turn around and I can't blame him.

I jump at the sound of his fist slamming into the metal door as he storms out of the kitchen, his angry departure ripping through my tattered heart.

The rest of the night passes in a blur of heartache. I avoid Tara's and Frank's concerned glances and wait for the bar to die down before leaving them to close up since they so graciously offered. By the time I climb into my car, I'm exhausted, both emotionally and physically, and wish for bed. Instead, I drive to the hospital.

The moment I walk through the sliding doors, I feel sick, my stomach churning at the pungent smell of disinfectant. I hate that she's here, hate that this is her home, but until I can afford us a house of our own and in-home care, this is where she needs to be.

I step onto the elevator, riding it up to the third floor. As I pass by the nurses' station, I greet Dina, the head nurse in charge.

"Hey, Zoey, do you have a minute?"

Concern has me coming to a hard stop. The only reason she would want to speak with me is if something happened.

"Is everything okay?"

"It is now."

My heart crawls into my throat as I wait for her to elaborate.

"She had another seizure today."

"How bad?"

Her long pause has icy cold fear flowing through my veins. "The worst one yet."

My eyes fall shut, defeat settling over me.

"She's okay now. Sleeping peacefully. The doctor will come speak with you in the morning. He's running more tests and wants to try her on a different medication."

"Okay. Thanks, Dina."

She puts a hand on my shoulder. "Hang in there, honey. Chrissy's strong and she's fighting."

As much as I appreciate her support, I find no comfort in her words. Because the truth of the matter is, Chrissy isn't strong and she hasn't been for a long time. Her condition continues to deteriorate no matter what we do and it leaves me feeling so helpless.

I continue to her room and open the door as quietly as possible. The dim light over her bed is on, casting a white glow on her as she lies fast asleep. Her mouth is open and body turned at an odd angle due to her muscle dysfunction.

The click of the door closing stirs her from her peaceful slumber. Her eyes flutter open, a noise working its way up her throat.

I walk forward, passing by her wheelchair and sit at the edge of her bed. "Hey, Chrissy Bee."

She stares up at me, a light entering her eyes that wasn't there a moment ago. When she looks at me like this, it gives me hope and eases some of my pain.

"D-D-Doey."

Happiness fills my chest to hear my name fall past her lips. She can't always say it. "Sorry to wake you. I meant to slip in quietly."

Her locked fingers grip mine in a strength that surprises me, her eyes conveying what she can't speak.

I know exactly what that look means. "Want me to stay tonight?"

Tremors rack her body as she blinks her answer at me.

"Okay," I whisper, trailing my finger down her soft cheek. Pulling my purse off my shoulder, I set it to the side and crawl in the bed behind her rather than sleep in the chair like I usually do. I have a feeling Chrissy needs me more than that tonight and if I'm being honest, I need her, too.

As I curl around my sister's broken body, smelling the subtle scent of her shampoo, I finally let the tears I've been holding in fall. Every one that spills is a prayer for Chrissy, that we find a way for her to live the life she deserves.

Never straying far from my mind and heart is the man I long for every night, wishing I could feel his strong arms around me now to hold all my broken pieces together.

CHAPTER FOUR

Austin

There's a grimness around the station that has never been present before. A heaviness and loss we all feel without Declan. It's been hanging over us like a dark cloud, darkening the mood of every person that walks in.

Usually, I love being here, this firehouse is my second home, residing my second family but right now I'm thankful the shift is almost over. It's been a long night with six calls, most of them car accidents. One that had a deceased mother and child that awaited us.

To finish off this clusterfuck of a night, we are now ending it by sitting in the conference room where Cap and Fire Investigator Roper go over the events of the warehouse explosion that took place. The entire house is here, right down to truck seventeen, my rescue squad, and paramedics.

They talk about what shouldn't have happened and what could have been done but one fact remains, one vital piece, and Cap is completely blunt, voicing what none of us have said yet.

"Declan would have made a great firefighter but he let his ego and eagerness override his sense. That one drastic move caused the backdraft and could have ended the lives of the other firefighters he was with."

It's something I've thought about often, how lucky the three of us are to still be here. It makes me as angry as it does Cap but then guilt soon follows. As much as it was a reckless decision on Declan's part, I can't help but wonder if there was more I could have done. As his lieutenant it was my job to lead him, teach him, and protect him.

"I've said this before and I will say it again, nothing is a priority if the risk is too great. Nothing. Do I make myself clear?"

"Yes, sir." Our collective answers fill the room, following a short span of silence.

"Good. You're dismissed. I'll see you all next shift."

Chairs scrape across the floor as everyone makes their exit.

"Hawke, Phillips, and Ryan," Cap calls just as we are about to walk out the door, "a word."

Jake, Cam, and I hold back, all of us exchanging a look.

Once the room is cleared, Roper closes the door, remaining with us.

Suspicion rears its ugly head. "What's going on?" I ask, looking directly at Cap.

"There's something you boys need to know before it goes public." He nods toward Roper to finish that statement.

"What we originally thought was an electrical fire due to the building not being up to code isn't the case. Traces of ethyl ether were found on scene."

"Son of a bitch!" Jake seethes, the fury in his hard tone matching the one coiling beneath my skin.

Ethyl ether is a highly flammable accelerant and sometimes can be hard to trace. It's bad enough to think of this as an unfortunate circumstance but now knowing it was intentional and cost Declan his life has a dark rage slipping over me.

"We're launching a full investigation."

"Suspects?" I ask.

"Not as of yet but that's not something you need to worry about. That's our job."

Jake tenses next to me, Roper's tone putting him on edge like the rest of us. Roper is an arrogant asshole, most of them over in arson are. They think they are better than the rest of us.

The truth is though, Jake's father was the best arson investigator there was, solving more cases than any other lead investigator in his time. How ironic it was that the very thing he out smarted took his life.

Roper never liked Jake's father, no doubt jealousy played a big role, which is why Jake was pissed as hell when the other man took over his father's position in the department.

"Look, I know this has been particularly hard on you boys," Cap says, breaking the tense silence. "As I said before, if you need more time…"

"I'm good," Jake says, quickly rejecting the offer.

Cam and I nod in agreement. The last thing I need is time off to dwell over what can't be changed, especially right now.

"Rest assured we will solve this and bring justice," Roper says, straightening his shoulders. "Chief Ramsey deserves it."

Remorse floods my veins as I think about how this must be affecting the chief. He's been through hell this past year. Despite Declan's reckless move, this bastard cost him his life. In my opinion there will never be any justice for that.

"Go home and get some rest," Cap says, ending the conversation as he heads for the door. "I'll see you boys tomorrow."

Roper shoots us a parting nod before following him out of the room.

"Well that was a swift kick to the balls," Cam rests back against the desk, his voice heavy with anger.

"I think Roper knows more than what he's saying," Jake says.

I have to agree, there was something in the other man's eyes, a knowledge he didn't share. Not that I'm surprised.

"Wanna speculate over breakfast?" Cam asks.

Jake shakes his head. "Can't. I need to get home and make sure Charlie's out of bed and on her way to school," he grumbles, talking about his teenage sister. "The last thing I need is any more calls from that damn counselor."

Charlie used to be so sweet and innocent but since the death of their parents and the aftermath of the fire she suffered with them, she's the definition of a teenage nightmare, making Jake pull out his hair every chance she gets. I feel for the poor bastard.

Cam looks to me but I opt out as well, needing to make a stop before I head home, one I have been avoiding.

"Fine. Suit yourselves. I'll just go get laid then and sleep the day away," he says, pushing from the desk. "Later."

"Later."

The two walk out together while I head to the locker room. On my way, I run into Mikey, a special needs boy who has been coming to this station for as long as I have worked here.

Cap lets him hang out once or twice a week. He helps around the station by cleaning and closing the overhead doors when we leave for a call. He loves it as much as we love having him around. He's a big part of our family, someone we all watch out for and respect.

"My man, Mikey." I stop him in the hallway, clapping him on the shoulder.

"Hey, Ausdin."

"Haven't seen you since we got back from that last call. Thanks for holding down the fort while we were gone."

His shoulders straighten, pride inflating his chest. "No problem."

"You headed home?"

He nods. "My ride will be here soon."

"Cool. I'll see you next week then."

"See ya."

I continue down the hall, entering the locker room only to come to a quick stop when I find Rubin Marks going through Declan's locker, mumbling to himself as he frantically searches for something.

"Hey."

He spins around, startled. "Lieutenant, I thought you left."

"I was just about to," I pause, assessing the rookie with narrowed eyes. "Everything okay?"

He clears his throat. "Yeah, fine."

My gaze shifts to the open locker he stands before. "What are you looking for?"

"Just something that I lent Declan last week." His expression sobers, pain slipping over his face. "Wow, last week." He drops down on the bench, shoulders slumping. "Hard to believe days ago he was here and now he's not."

I walk over and take a seat next to him. "It's hard to accept, isn't it?"

He nods. "Really hard."

Declan's death has been hard on us all but especially Rubin. They both graduated from the academy together and became really good friends in and out of this station.

"Can't help but feel like it's my fault. If I hadn't asked him to switch shifts with me…" His words trail off, leaving a grim silence with them.

Rubin was supposed to be with us that night, but in a sick twist of fate he asked Declan to cover his shift because of a family gathering. I can understand why he'd feel blame, hell, I feel a lot of it but no one knew what could have come from that one decision.

"Don't do this to yourself. You heard what Cap said. This isn't on you."

He remains silent, refusing to hear the words.

"This is the job, man. Honor Declan for it. Remember him that way."

He nods but I know, like me, it's going to take time.

"Should I request to bring the chaplain in for you?"

He shakes his head. "Nah. I'm good." Picking up his bag, he stands and closes Declan's locker. "Thanks for the talk, Lieutenant. I'll see you next shift." Without another word, he walks out.

I gaze back at the locker before me, and despite the pep talk I just gave Rubin, the guilt inflating my chest threatens to swallow me whole.

It's then I make my own exit. Before going home though, I drive to see the woman I walked out on the other night, the same one whose pretty sad blue eyes torment me on the darkest nights.

CHAPTER FIVE

Zoey

The morning sun shines with promise as I walk out of my apartment building with my travel mug in one hand and purse hanging from the other. Despite my lack of sleep, the warmth on my skin gives me a sense of hope for the coming day.

I'm anxious to see Chrissy and pray the new meds the doctor put her on are still working. Her tremors are worse, a common side effect, but she is more alert and her muscle movement has slightly improved. Yesterday, she even cracked a smile. I will take the small feat.

Just as I round the corner toward my car, my feet falter at the truck I find parked on the side of the street. I would know that truck anywhere.

My heart stutters when Austin climbs out, holding a bouquet of daffodils and looking as devastatingly handsome as always. His expression is solemn, eyes shielded by aviators as he starts toward me.

"Hey." His deep voice slides over every inch of my skin, warming me from the inside out.

"Hey," I reply softly. "You're out and about early."

"Just finished my shift."

I nod, hope and fear colliding in my chest as I wonder what brought him here.

Without another word, he passes me the bouquet.

"What are these for?" The question leaves me as I lift them to my nose, the soft aroma bringing a smile to my face.

"An apology." Remorse enters his voice. "I'm sorry for walking out on you the other night. I was drunk and pissed off."

My gaze drops, pain infiltrating my chest. I don't blame him for being angry with me. Everything he said the other night is true. I shut him out, even as a friend.

"I miss you," I confess, feeling vulnerable as the words leave my mouth. "I miss seeing you around the bar."

He reaches out, touching the side of my face. "Me too, Zoey girl."

I lean into his touch, craving the simple contact from him.

"How about breakfast?" he asks, before quickly adding, "as friends."

Regret crashes down on me but I mask it with an apologetic smile. "I'm actually just on my way over to the hospital to see my sister. I want to get some time in with her before work."

"I understand. Another time then." Leaning down, he drops the softest kiss at the corner of my eye, the whisper of a touch reaching far more than skin deep.

Just as he steps back, I grab his arm. "Would you like to come?" The offer is out of my mouth before I can even think about it but as I ask the question, it feels right.

Surprise flares in his eyes. "Really?"

I nod. "I'd like you to meet her."

None of my friends have met my sister, except Sam. Usually because she isn't in any condition for visitors, but on this new medication, I feel confident she can handle it. I'm ready to share this part of my life with him.

His silence has me feeling unsure.

"I know you're just getting off shift. So if you're too tired we can do it another time or—"

"I'd love to meet her, Zoey." He slings an arm around my shoulders, pulling me into his side and gracing me with that sexy smirk of his. "Come on. I'll drive then take you to the bar after."

"Okay." I walk tucked into his side, his body heat enveloping me.

The short fifteen-minute trip is filled with small talk as we catch up on all the things we've missed with each other. It's easy, comfortable even. Like we never missed a beat. It gives me hope that maybe, just maybe, we can get back the friendship we had.

The easy moment changes when we enter the hospital, nerves dancing in my belly. It makes me feel vulnerable to show him this part of my life but I'm hoping once he sees her, meets her, he will understand why I can't commit to having anything more. No matter how much I wish otherwise.

Dina greets us as we walk off the elevator. "Well, you're here bright and early."

"I'm going into work earlier today. How is she doing?"

"Wonderful," she tells me, her smile bringing truth to the words. "She had a great night and so far a very good morning. She was even able to hold her breakfast spoon."

The information sends joy exploding through my heart. "That's amazing. She hasn't been able to do that in so long."

"I know. This medication so far is doing wonders. I think we finally found something that works for her."

I let go of a relieved sigh, feeling like the world has been lifted off my shoulders. She still has a long ways to go but this is a start. A very good start.

Dina's eyes move to Austin and there is no denying the appreciation in them. Can't say I blame her, he's easy to look at.

"This is my friend Austin," I say, introducing him. "I brought him along to meet Chrissy."

"Nice to meet you, Austin," she returns, extending her hand. "I'm Dina, the head nurse in charge."

"Nice to meet you, as well."

Her eyes narrow for a fraction of a second. "I recognize you. Have you been here before?"

"I've been in the emergency quite a few times with the fire department."

"That's right," she says, realization dawning on her. "You're with Fire Station Two. Captain Gyepesi's crew."

"That's correct."

"Austin's station is also the one who did the charity event to raise money for the center," I tell her.

A grateful smile takes over her face. "Well, thank you for that. We are always in need of donations and it makes a difference for our patients."

"Anything for Zoey," he says, looking down at me in a way that has butterflies dancing in my belly. I cling to the feeling, getting lost in his warm brown eyes, as if the irises hold all the answers I've been looking for.

Dina clears her throat, yanking me back to reality.

I give my head a mental shake for the silly thought. "Do you think she's well enough for us to take her for a walk outside?"

"I think she would love that. Just let me clear it with Dr. Carver first. Go on and I'll let you know when I speak with him."

"Thanks."

I lead Austin down the hall, anticipation fueling each step. I'm even more anxious to see her now, to see these results with my own eyes. Opening the door to her room, I find her sitting up in her wheelchair, facing the window. This sight alone is improvement.

"Hey, Chrissy Bee." I walk around to the front of her chair, knowing she isn't strong enough to turn her head, and see she's holding her favorite stuffed animal.

"D-Doey." Despite the tremors, there's that same light in her eyes that's always there.

"Nurse Dina tells me you've had a good morning."

"Ve-ry go-ood." Her eyes move to Austin as he comes to stand next to me, curiosity adopting her face.

"Chrissy, I want you to meet a good friend of mine, Austin. Austin, this is my sister, Chrissy."

He crouches down before her, taking her small hand racked with tremors into his large one. "Nice to meet you, Chrissy. I see you're just as beautiful as your sister."

A light blush stains her cheeks, the slightest hint of a smile playing at the edge of her lips. Her eyes come back to mine. "B-B-Boyfrie-end?" The question ends on a giggle and it triggers my own.

"No. Not boyfriend. Just friend."

I've never felt more like a liar than I do now, because what I feel for this man is so much more than friendship. If only circumstances were different...

"Too bad for me, isn't it?" Austin jokes, making her giggle again. "Who's this?" he asks, reaching out to touch the stuffed yellow Labrador she holds.

"G-us," she answers.

"Cool name for a cool dog."

"Chrissy and I have always wanted a dog like this one," I confess. "When she comes to live with me, we're going to make that happen, aren't we Chrissy?"

She doesn't respond with her usual excitement. Her attention is anchored on Austin, studying him in a way I've never seen her do before. It's then I notice her eyes on the crest of his jacket.

"He's a firefighter," I tell her.

"He-ero."

Austin quickly shakes his head but I don't let him deny it, my hand moving to his shoulder.

"Yes. He is."

His eyes meet mine over his shoulder, that ever-present pull passing between us. He has no idea just how many times he has saved me from darkness, from my own personal guilt and despair.

Our moment is broken when Dina walks into the room with the okay from the doctor. "A new playground was built out in the left sector," she says. "There's a swing she can be strapped into if you want to take her there. It should be fairly quiet right now. If you need help lifting her, I can send an orderly."

"No," Austin declines. "We got her."

We. How less alone one word can make someone feel.

Dina nods, her attention coming back to me. "Just make sure you're back by lunch. Dr. Carver will be doing his rounds after that."

"Thanks, Dina."

After she leaves, I grab Chrissy a sweater from her closet, putting her arms through it. Despite the warm weather, there's a slight breeze and she doesn't have good circulation.

Austin grabs the door as I wheel my sister out of the room and into the elevator. The moment we step outside into the sunshine, a noise leaves Chrissy's throat, an almost sigh drifting among the breeze.

I look around the chair and into her face. "Good?"

"N-n-ice."

It's something that most people take for granted. Even I have come to learn that getting to feel the sun on your skin or breathing in the outdoor air is a privilege, among many other things Chrissy misses out on daily.

We come up to the playground Dina told us about and find it empty. A large seat with black straps hangs in the middle between two others. I push Chrissy's chair close enough and begin unstrapping her before Austin steps in.

"I got her." He bends down, lifting her out of the chair and into his arms.

My heart stops, a moment in time coming to a standstill. Seeing my sister's broken body in his strong arms is one of the most breathtaking sights I've ever seen.

By the color that invades her cheeks, I'd say she likes it, too. "S-S-trong," she says.

"No way. You're a lightweight."

He straps her in and I'm about to walk behind her but Austin does first, gently pushing her. A choppy giggle leaves her, drifting through the air and filling my heart.

I take a seat, watching as Chrissy's eyes close. The breeze hits her face, a hint of a smile touching her lips. It's been so long since I've seen her happy. It has me reaching for my phone and snapping a picture, wanting to capture this moment forever, to remember this look on her face when the hard days emerge. Where there is no pain, no frustration or sadness, only...peace.

"Come here, Zoey." Austin's deep voice drags my attention away from my sister. He nods at the swing next to her. "I'll push you, too."

Smiling, I walk over and take a seat, lifting my feet as Austin gives me gentle pushes the same way he does my sister. I reach for Chrissy's hand, taking it in mine and embracing a moment I've never been able to have with her. A moment that sisters should always share at some point in their lives, but we were robbed of it because of the hand we were dealt.

I look over my shoulder, my breath halting when I find Austin watching me. He looks at me in a way no one else has before, like I'm the center of his universe when usually I feel like I'm nothing more than a lost soul in a sea of bodies.

The rest of the morning consists of beautiful memories that I will hold in my heart forever and it's two hours later when we take Chrissy back to her room. We stay with her while she eats her lunch then tuck her in for a nap, all the fresh air wearing her out.

I drop down, giving her my usual kiss on the cheek. "I'll be back late tonight."

She nods before shifting her eyes to Austin behind me. "Y-ou co-me baack?"

"Definitely." He takes her hand in his, bringing it to his lips for a kiss. "It was nice to meet you, Chrissy. Thanks for letting me hang out with you and your sister today."

We leave her with a smile on her face, one I will carry with me for the rest of the day.

On the drive over to the bar, I reflect on the last few hours and how amazing Austin was with my sister—how gentle and sweet he was with her. Not that I'm surprised, I always knew he would be accepting of her. I just never expected for it to feel so right.

It isn't long before he pulls up to the bar, parking along the street, and I'm sad our time has come to an end.

I finally look over at him, resting my head back against the seat. "Do you understand now? Do you see how much she needs me and why I need to be there for her?"

"I always understood it, Zoey. I never faulted you for it. I just want to walk it with you. Whether it's as a friend or more."

I wish he understood just how much I want that too, but I also don't want him to shoulder any responsibility, and I know he would. That's just the kind of man he is—good, kind, and compassionate.

I don't like to think of my sister as a responsibility because she isn't, but her disability is and it can be draining.

"I had fun today," he continues.

"I did too but it's not always like that," I whisper. "Today was a good day, but most aren't like this. Most are hard and painful, especially for Chrissy."

"You think I'm going to just bail when things get tough?"

Everyone else has... I manage to bite my tongue and refrain from saying that out loud.

He lets go of a frustrated breath. "Tell me to mind my own business but where are your parents in all this?"

A rush of emotions explode to the surface, the most prominent one being anger. "My father abandoned us when I was fifteen, Chrissy was only a newborn. I have no idea where he is, and my mother,"—my teeth grind as I think about her—"she's never given a damn. The only thing she cares about is drowning herself in the next bottle and boyfriend."

The hatred that always bubbles up when I think of the woman who birthed me threatens to spill over. How a mother can just check out on her kids, especially when it comes to Chrissy, is beyond me, but I gave up trying to figure her out a long time ago.

"It's always been just Chrissy and I for the most part."

"I'm sorry," he says.

"Don't be. We have each other and that's all that matters."

He reaches for my hand, taking it in his large one. "You have me, too," he says, making my heart swell in my chest. "I'm not going anywhere, Zoey. I'll always be here for you. No matter what."

I shake my head, feeling so undeserving of this man. "Why do you waste so much time on me?"

"You say it's a waste, I say it's time well spent." His words are like a soothing balm, blanketing my soul. "Even if you are stubborn as hell."

A smile eases on my lips as I enjoy this lighter moment with him. "It's a gift," I tease.

He grunts but lifts my hand to his mouth, kissing the inside of my wrist. "Thank you for letting me meet her."

Taking off my seatbelt, I reach over the console and press a kiss to his jaw, letting my lips linger as I fight the urge to give him so much more. "Go get some sleep, Hawke, before you wear down all the reasons why this isn't a good idea."

"In that case, I'll be back later."

A giggle escapes me as I jump out of his truck. "Bye."

"Later, Zoey girl."

Closing the door, I walk inside the bar, wishing more than anything I was walking toward the man who owns my heart rather than away from him.

CHAPTER SIX

Austin

Adrenaline pumps through my blood, our sirens piercing the air as the fire truck speeds through the night. We blow through red lights, forcing vehicles to slam on their brakes, making the entire world around us come to a stop.

In this moment, nothing else matters but this call and the lives we will potentially save.

Orange flames roar in the distance, lighting up the dark sky as we approach the blazing apartment building.

"Jesus, she's fucking raging," Cam murmurs, ducking to get a better look out the window.

Tenants from the building stand across the street, watching the scene unfold as we pull up. Truck seventeen parks behind us while Cap comes to a screeching stop directly beside us, assessing the inferno.

The second we jump out to join him, a man comes running over in a frantic state. "I'm the manager," he tells us, his words rushed and panicked. "It came out of nowhere. I have no idea what could have started it."

"Is everyone out?" I ask.

He nods. "I think so."

I watch the dancing flames, trying to gauge their direction while Cap starts passing out orders. Then it happens, the subtle scent penetrates my senses, sinking into the pit of my stomach. It's one I could never forget.

"Cap, the smell," I say, looking over at him.

I don't have to elaborate, he knows what I'm talking about. It took one of our own.

His chin lifts as he takes his own whiff of smoke-filled air. "You sure it's the same?"

"It is," Jake says without hesitation.

"All right, we fight this on the outside, no one goes inside that building, understand?"

We all nod, springing into action when a piercing cry shatters the night. A woman with tears streaming down her face runs straight for us. "Help me! Please, my boy is still inside! He's only nine."

An iron fist grips my chest to think of anyone in that blazing fury, let alone a child. "What floor?"

"Third. Apartment 302. He left with us. I know he did," she cries. "He was right behind his brother and sister. I don't know what happened."

I turn to Cap, ready to plead my case. "Let us go. Cam, Jake, and I can cover a large area in a short amount of time."

Indecision wars on his face, the risk after what we endured the other week still fresh. "You have exactly three minutes," he decides. "If I call it sooner you get the hell out of there. No questions asked. Understand?"

"Yes, sir."

We waste no time masking up and moving for the building, these next few minutes imperative for not only us but also the little boy inside.

"Marks, Fuller, and Duggar," I call into my radio. "I want each of you stationed on each side of the building. Be ready if we need to come out a window."

"Copy that, Lieutenant."

"We each take a floor," I speak to Cam and Jake next. "Phillips, you take first, Ryan, you take second. I got the third."

Their silence is all I need as compliance as we move in unison. We have fought side by side long enough that we know how the other works.

Moments later, we enter the raging depths of hell. The only other monster I've seen of this magnitude is the one we barely made it out of alive the other week. Regardless of the crushing thought, none of us falter.

Cam claps my shoulder as he enters further in, covering his designated area.

We barely hear his muffled calls as Jake and I take the stairs two at a time, pushing through the thick black smoke while flames threaten to engulf us at every angle. Jake takes a left on the second floor, leaving me to continue to the third. Once at the top, I crouch low, shoving my way through the fiery chaos with thermal imaging.

"Fire department, call out!" I listen for any signs of life; opening every cracked door I pass. Each time I'm met with nothing but sweeping flames.

"Hawke, report," Cap bellows through the radio.

I press the button on my mic. "No sign yet but I still have half the floor to cover. I'm on the east side now."

"You have less than two minutes. This smoke is taking a quick direction. I don't like it."

Teeth grinding, I push myself harder, blinking through the sweat dripping into my eyes and breathing the filtering oxygen into my lungs.

"First floor is clear," Cam reports. "I'm coming up to help with the second."

Just then I push open another cracked door and encounter something. Reaching inside, relief courses through me as my fingers grip a small ankle. "I got him!"

I crawl over top to get a better look, shielding the small boy from the chaos around us. My gut tightens as I take in his blackened arm and the raw flesh exposed on the left side of his neck.

He stares up at me helplessly, a single tear escaping his eye, sliding down his rounded cheek. "Help me," he mouths, the words never making it past his throat.

"It's going to be all right, buddy. Hang in there. I'm going to get you out of here." I press my chest for the mic. "Cap. Have paramedics waiting and ready."

"Copy. Now get out of there. All of you." The concern in his steely command is unmistakable.

We're running out of time.

I slip off my mask and hold it over the boy's small face. My lungs immediately react, burning like an inferno as I inhale nothing but the black smoke billowing around me.

Cradling the young body in my arms, I climb to my feet, determination fueling each hurried step. My strides are quick, eyes burning as I take the stairs.

Jake and Cam meet us halfway up the stairs. They cover either side of me, offering the boy more of a shield from the suffocating heat. Jake slips his mask off and holds it to my face. I take in a few lungfuls of clean air before pushing it back in his direction.

"Let's go!"

As we make it to the first floor, the roof starts to break, causing pieces of wood and debris to rain down around us.

"Squad five. Out now!" The roar comes from Captain just as we reach the front door. "It's about to flash."

All of us break into a run, heat roaring at our backs, reaching for us, threatening to claim.

I duck at the explosion, making it to the street before turning around to watch the building crumble into nothing but rubble. All of it incinerating in the blink of an eye.

"Isaiah!"

The boy's mother runs for us as I help the waiting paramedics load the small child onto the gurney.

"Oh god," she sobs when she sees the condition he's in, falling to her knees. "Please, God. Not my baby."

The boy's eyes barely flutter open as my mask is removed and replaced with oxygen. His dark gaze locks with mine, saying everything he can't. The tortured pain there strikes me in the chest. The depth of his wounds will be scars he will carry for the rest of his life, if he pulls through at all. The thought that he might not is unthinkable.

"Nice job, Lieutenant," Duggar says, clapping my shoulder, though he looks at all three of us. "Seems like you guys have nine lives lately."

The joke is amiss. Cam, Jake, and I share a grim look, knowing we once again escaped death by precious seconds.

This was no accident.

If we don't find out who's doing this, and soon, there's no telling what will be at stake next.

CHAPTER SEVEN

Zoey

The late night rush has just started to settle, my aching feet a cold reminder that I need more help around here, but with more help comes more pay and I need all the money I can get right now, especially with this new drug Chrissy is on. I'm paying more out of pocket than ever before, but it's worth it.

She's worth it.

I will walk a thousand steps, wait on a thousand tables, and exhaust myself to no end in order to make sure my sister gets the help she needs.

Despite the financial hardship lately, nothing can dull the happiness in my heart that's been growing every day since that morning with Austin and my sister.

He has come to see me every day since then. Sometimes only for a few short minutes before shift and other times he stays longer, tempting me with that sexy smirk and good boy charm.

He always leaves me with a kiss on the cheek, one that I feel for hours after. It leaves my lips burning in mourning and regret, wishing they could feel that explosive touch just one more time.

He's slowly wearing me down and he knows it. All the reasons I've been telling myself of why I don't think we are a good idea doesn't seem to matter anymore. It's dangerous for my carefully guarded heart.

"Still got that smile I see," Frank remarks from behind the bar, a knowing look in his eyes.

"Smile?" I feign ignorance.

It makes the older man chuckle. "You know what I'm talking about.

Clearly that man is on your mind again."

Busted.

"It's a pretty smile, sweetheart. You should carry it around more often."

The light moment becomes heavy with the truth. I hate to think how sad I look most of the time. Mainly because I am. Some days it's really hard to remain upbeat when my sister is constantly fighting for her life, but I need to do better at it, not only for my sake but everyone else's around me. I need to appreciate the things we do have going for us rather than what we don't.

I decide to start right now. Lifting to the tips of my toes, I bend over the counter and give him a kiss on the cheek.

The older man's dark face reddens. "What was that for?"

"For being you. Thank you for being here and helping so much. I couldn't do it without you."

He shrugs off my gratitude. "Get outta here, kid. This is all you. I'm just glad you let me come along for the ride. Besides,"—he pauses, clearing his throat—"being here is good for me, too. Stops me from being home alone and in my head. Trust me, nothing good ever comes from that."

Being a veteran, I can't even imagine what memories haunt him. I do, however, know what it's like to not want to walk into the darkness of your own thoughts. If being here helps silence his demons, then here he will stay.

"I'll keep you around for as long as you want me, Frank."

"You ain't ever getting rid of me, sweetheart." He finishes that vow with a wink, igniting a warmth in my chest. I have more friends than I realize, it's been hard to remember that since Sam moved away.

As happy as I am for her to be living her dreams over in South Carolina, I've missed her. She's always been my biggest confidant. We've known each other since junior high. She's been with me through some of my hardest obstacles and so has her family. If not for her father, I wouldn't even own this bar. He helped me with start-up costs so I would have income to take care of Chrissy after my mother bailed.

When Sam and I do have time to talk, I never want to bore her with my problems. Lately, we chat about her upcoming wedding, something I'm so excited for. To know she's coming back here for it is even better, especially since funds are low right now and the thought of leaving Chrissy for only a few days doesn't sit well with me.

I'm honored she asked me to be her maid of honor and with Austin being Jase's best man it means we will be walking that aisle together. The thought triggers an almost giddy sensation inside of me. It makes me even more excited for our friends' upcoming nuptials.

"Hey, Zoey?" Tara walks over to where we are at the bar, hands fidgeting. Her visible nerves instantly put me on alert.

"Yeah?"

"There's someone here to see you."

When her gaze shifts over my shoulder, I turn around, shock rooting me to my spot at the woman standing just inside the bar. It's been over a year since I have seen or spoken to my mother.

My wide eyes drift over her, taking in her worn appearance. I resemble this woman more than I care to admit, but where my long sun-kissed hair is clean and wavy, hers is dirty and tied back. My blue eyes are clear and hers are clouded with whatever she's on at the moment.

It doesn't take long before the shock lifts and anger quickly takes its place. I waste no time walking up to her, my fingernails biting into my palms.

She shoots me a nervous smile. "Hey, baby. You're looking good."

"What are you doing here?" I ask, forgoing all pleasantries.

"Can't I come by and see how my daughter is doing?"

"You could but it's been a year and you have another daughter who needs you more."

Her lips press into a thin line at the mention of Chrissy. "Look, I know it's been a while. Things have been…hard lately."

She doesn't know the meaning, because anytime life gets hard, she bails.

"I didn't come here to fight. Can we talk for a minute, please?"

I contemplate kicking her out, not caring what she has to say, but my curiosity ends up getting the best of me and I gesture to one of the tables in the far corner. She heads that way, leaving the scent of vodka in her wake.

Her gaze moves around the bar as she takes a seat. "The place looks great. Business good?"

I shrug. "It pays medical bills."

Her chin juts out, eyes narrowing. "Why do you always do that?"

"Do what?"

"Throw your sister in my face."

It's on the tip of my tongue to tell her she has two daughters, one of whom needs her constant care and attention, but I bite back my retort. Chrissy and I don't matter to her. I often wonder if we ever did.

"Say what you want, Mother, then get out of here."

She lifts her hands in front of her, surrendering. "All right. Fine. We'll do this your way." She pauses, her bottom lip trembling.

I barely refrain from rolling my eyes. She has always been a great actress.

"Jerry and I broke up," she blurts out.

I stare back at her, wondering why she thinks I care. I didn't even know she'd been dating a guy named Jerry.

"He ran out one night, taking pretty much everything I owned, and never came back." The words are delivered on a sad whisper but I have no sympathy for her.

"Well, Mom, maybe it's time you clean yourself up and stop shacking up with losers."

Her shoulders stiffen, face pinching in anger. The façade is slipping, just like I knew it would. "I'm trying here, Zoey. I just...I need some help to get me back on my feet."

Her motive for being here finally dawns on me, a bitter laugh escaping my mouth. "You're unbelievable."

"It would be just a small loan," she rushes to say. "I'll pay you back once I get my life in order."

"How dare you," I snap, my voice carrying through the bar but I'm too angry to care. "How dare you come here and ask me for money when I can barely afford to take care of my sister!"

"I want to get better, Zoey. For you and Chrissy."

"Bullshit! I fell for that once before and I never will again."

A few years back I managed to scrounge up five thousand dollars to give her because she promised she was going to get clean and become a better mother. It never happened. She used it for booze and drugs.

"I mean it this time. I've even been looking into rehab centers and—"

"You smell like alcohol right now. Always solving your problems with a bottle, isn't that right, Mother?"

"Says the woman who owns a bar," she fires back.

"This bar pays for Chrissy's medical bills. Ones you left solely on my shoulders."

"What do you expect?" she cries. "You want to know why I am the way I am? Take a good long look at your sister. Do you have any idea how hard it was to take care of her?"

"Yeah, Mom. I have a really good idea. I've been doing it since I was a child."

"Oh please, Zoey. You're always feeling sorry for yourself. You didn't have to pick up the financial responsibility. The state would have put her up in that hospital and neither of us would have had to pay a cent. You chose to take that problem on yourself."

"She's not a problem, Mother. She is a human being. My sister. *Your* daughter!" Tears sting my eyes as I think about the unfairness of this all, especially for Chrissy. "She's a bright, beautiful girl who deserves to be loved as much as anyone else. We both do and you never gave it to us!" My hands slam down on the table as my temper takes hold. "You are crazy if you think I will give you a dime. All the money I make goes to my sister."

"I'm your mother!"

"You are nothing of the sort. Not to me or Chrissy. Now get the hell out of my bar and don't come back."

She pushes from the table to stand, knocking the chair over in her anger and points down at me. "Both of you were the biggest mistakes of my life, just like your father was."

The hurtful lashing is not a surprise, but all the same, the cruel words rip through my chest, slicing my soul deep.

"You need help over here, Zoey?" Frank comes to stand next to me, his hand grasping my shoulder as he glares at my mother.

I reach for his comfort, needing it to mask the cold pain thrumming through my veins. A pain I should no longer be feeling when it comes to this woman.

"No, Frank. That's all right. She was just leaving."

My mother spins on her heels, an angry cry fleeing from her as she storms out of the bar. It isn't until the door slams shut behind her that I take in my first full breath but it's a painful one, making it difficult to breathe.

"You all right, sweetheart?" Frank asks, sympathy laced in his voice.

I nod since I can't manage words. Swallowing thickly, I finally find them. "Do you mind closing up? I really need to go see my sister right now."

"Of course. You go on. Tara and I got this."

"Thanks." After giving his hand a gentle squeeze, I grab my stuff and leave, thankful to see my mother nowhere in sight.

On the drive over, her hurtful words replay, reminding me of the abandonment she inflicted upon Chrissy and me. All the times I had to come up with some lie to tell my sister as to why our mother just disappeared from our lives and why she never comes to see her in the hospital. Now she has the audacity to come and ask me for money when I'm barely making ends meet as it is.

The thought has my hurt quickly morphing into anger.

By the time I arrive at the hospital, I'm raging. I head up to the third floor, ignoring the looks from strangers as they stare at my hot face. My sandals furiously click down the hall as I head toward my sister.

The moment I step into her room, I find Austin sitting next to her bed. I blink several times, shocked to find him here.

"D-oey!" my sister greets me, excitement laced in my name.

My eyes remain on Austin as he stands. He's in his turnout gear, smelling like smoke, his face dirty with soot. Despite all that, he looks as handsome as ever.

"What are you doing here?" I ask, fearing something has happened.

"I was in the area and thought I would stop by to say hi to Chrissy." He nudges her chin gently, smiling down at her.

The way she stares up at him, wide-eyed and fixated, brings a cold realization. She's becoming attached—too attached. He shouldn't be doing this. It's not fair. Not to her or me.

"Can I talk to you outside for a minute?" I'm unable to mask the bite in my tone and he senses it.

After a nod in my direction, he looks down at my sister again, flashing her that smirk of his. "I'll see you later, pretty girl."

Her cheeks turn pink at the compliment. "B-ye, Aus-din."

I follow him out the door, feeling myself drowning in mixed emotions.

He wastes no time turning on me, crossing his arms over his chest. "What's the problem, Zoey?"

"You shouldn't be here," I tell him, hating the words as soon as they leave my mouth.

"Why?"

"She's getting too attached."

"I just stopped in to say hi. What's wrong with that?"

"Everything is wrong with that," I snap. "What happens when the time comes that you walk away? Who is going to explain that to her then?"

"Who said anything about walking away?"

"No one else has ever stuck around, why would you?"

He straightens, frustration masking his expression. "I thought we were past this, Zoey."

"So did I but you keep pushing. At every turn, there you are, interjecting yourself when I keep telling you *I can't do this*. It isn't fair!"

His warm brown eyes shut out any emotion but anger. He takes a step forward, his furious face inches before mine. "No. What you're doing isn't fair. Let's be honest, you aren't protecting your sister. You're protecting yourself because *you* are scared."

I grind my teeth at the truth he says, a truth I can't face.

"You isolate yourself from anyone who tries to get close and I'm fucking tired of it. You want me gone? Fine, have it your way. I'm out of here."

Before I even have a chance to apologize and make things right, he's gone, leaving my already mangled heart bleeding on the floor.

CHAPTER EIGHT

Austin

My hammer is heavy and hard as I furiously drive a nail into another board, practically putting a fucking hole through it. The blistering sun has started to descend but I'm not ready to quit for the day. I still have too much aggression to work out.

It's been almost twenty-four hours since my run-in with Zoey and I'm no less pissed off than I was last night. I'm angry at her...angry at myself.

I've been living here for a month now and I'm constantly reminded of the unforgettable night I spent with the girl who left before the morning sun, leaving her memory behind and scent lingering on my skin.

I should have backed off then but it's hard when I know how much she wants this. I see it in the way she looks at me, with the same need and longing I have for her.

I went to the hospital last night to check on the little boy I pulled from the fire, unable to get his scared, pleading eyes out of my head. After seeing him and finding out he would pull through despite his extensive injuries, I stopped in to see Chrissy. I needed something good to finish off the night. I didn't think it would be a big deal.

Clearly, I was wrong.

Teeth grinding, I go grab the last board from the bed of my truck, laying into it the same way I have all the others. I'm done playing hot and cold. Zoey wants me gone, I'm gone. For good.

The ache that thought brings on is fierce but I shove it away, allowing my anger to override all else. It hurts a hell of a lot less...

Minutes later, a car drives down the long gravel road that leads to my house. Looking over my shoulder, I blink the sweat away and find it's none other than the woman who's wreaking havoc on my patience and cock.

Zoey steps out of the car and the shift I get in my chest at the sight of her in a simple yellow sundress makes me want to kick myself in the face. She looks innocent, sweet...vulnerable. It pisses me off even more which is why I return to my task at hand and ignore her.

"Hey," she greets with that soft voice of hers, walking up behind me.

Bang.

Bang.

Bang.

"I called you earlier."

Bang.

Bang.

Bang.

"I also left a message."

Bang.

Bang.

Bang.

"You wouldn't happen to be pretending it's my face you're hammering right now, are you?" Amusement coats her tone as she attempts the joke.

I want to hammer her all right but not the way she's thinking...

I leave that thought unfinished and continue to ignore her even though I really want to turn around and kiss the shit out of her.

I'm fucking pathetic.

Just then I send the hammer into my thumb like an asshole, inflicting excruciating pain. "Goddamn it. Motherfucker, piece of shit!" I throw the hammer across the yard then kick the board before turning to face the woman I'm really pissed off at. "What do you want?"

She takes a step back, swallowing nervously. "I came to apologize."

"Save it. I don't want to hear it." I stomp across the yard, needing to put some distance between us before I do something really stupid. Like cave to those blue irises.

"Please, give me the chance to explain."

I whip around, finding her right behind me. "Explain what, Zoey? How you're always pushing me away? How you use me as your punching bag when you need to let off some steam? Or maybe you're sorry about the way you use your sister as a crutch so you don't have to face your own shit."

It's a low blow and I know it. The pain that washes over her face strikes my angry heart like a carving knife.

She shakes her head. "Never mind. This was a mistake." She turns her back on me, fleeing for her car, but there's no chance in hell I'm letting her run away.

Not this time.

"I don't think so, baby." I charge after her, my fingers gripping her arm as I whirl her back around to face me. "You came all this way for something. What is it? Tell me what you fucking want from me."

"Your friendship!" she wails.

"Well maybe I can't be your friend anymore, Zoey. Not when you're constantly looking at me like you want me to fuck you all the time."

Her eyes narrow at the truth, one she refuses to accept. "You're such an asshole."

She tries to pull away but I yank her closer. My hard cock presses into her stomach, begging for any part of her. Her pretty pink lips part, cheeks flushing from anger and desire, the same emotions roaring through my veins.

"Tell me you don't want this," I say, my face only an inch from hers. "Tell me right now that you don't want me the same way I do you and I'll drop it for good. I will work past these feelings and be nothing but your friend."

She gazes up at me, her eyes conveying what I already know. What I have always known. "It's not that simple."

"The hell it isn't!"

"I have responsibilities, Austin! People I need to put before myself. Why can't you understand that?"

"Stop using her as an excuse!"

"Why should I get to be happy when she'll never be?" she yells, finally laying out the truth. "She will never get to love someone. She will never get to feel someone's loving touch. So why the hell should I?" The last of her words fall on a heartbreaking sob. "It should have been me. She doesn't deserve this."

I quickly realize this is far more than fear. She's punishing herself.

"Zoey..." I trail off, shaking my head.

"You always do this. You always push!" She lashes out, her fists striking my bare chest in a fit of rage. "Fuck you for making this harder on us both!"

I grab her wrists, stopping the attack, and seize her mouth with my own, claiming what I can't bring myself to let go, to set free from the imprisonment she has over me.

Her response is quick, fingers spearing through my hair. It's the match to the gasoline, igniter to my flame, throwing us into a combustible heat. When her teeth nip my lip, hard enough to draw blood, I become unhinged.

Growling, I reach down and hoist her up. Her legs lock around my waist, hot center grinding against my stomach.

"Tell me you want it," I demand, my mouth never faltering its assault.

"I want it." The words fall on nothing more than a breathless whisper but the impact they carry, the truth they hold, fall upon my ears like the sweetest fucking symphony.

Within a few steps, I have her on her back on a dirty blanket in the bed of my truck. I reach under her dress, ripping her satin panties from her hips while she works on my belt.

Once my cock is freed, she eagerly guides me to her entrance, our bodies both moving for the other's, reaching for that mind-numbing pleasure that will destroy us both. The moment I drive in, she thrusts up, burying me to the hilt.

"Fuck me!" My head drops back on my shoulders, swimming with pleasure as my entire fucking world is rocked for a second time.

"Austin, please." The desperate plea quivers past her lips, her need colliding with my own.

I fuck her hard and fast, releasing the desire I have burning in my soul. One that rages only for her. Her back arches, fingers gripping the blanket over her head while mine sink into her hips. I give her everything we have both wanted since that first night. What she's so hellbent on fighting.

The reminder has my anger rushing back to the surface. "You feel this, Zoey?" I ask on a growl. "You feel how fucking right this is? This is what you're denying us both!"

Regret flashes in her eyes, mixing with the desire. "I'm sorry," she chokes out.

I still deep inside of her, her grief changing the moment entirely. Leaning down, I brush my lips against hers, tasting her tears. "Don't cry, baby."

She wraps her arms around my neck, hugging me close. "I want this. I want *you*. So much."

"I'm yours, Zoey. I always have been, all you have to do is take me."

A moment of truth passes between us as I remain seated deep inside her. Her hands move to my face, pulling my mouth down to hers, taking what she's been so afraid to admit. I drink her pain and fear, inhaling it as my own, and pick up where I left off, my cock pumping hard and deep.

Her breath races against my lips as she rides the edge of destruction I'm so desperate to keep her on.

"Austin." There's fear in her voice as she fights the orgasm trying to claim her.

"I got you, Zoey girl. Let go. I promise to catch you."

Our gazes lock, mine begging for trust and hers seeking redemption. I finally win. Her eyes drift shut as she falls blindly into pleasure.

Heat licks down my spine, my jaw locking and teeth grinding as I fight like hell to hold back. "Are you on the pill, Zoey?"

Her eyes spring open, clouded with ecstasy. "Yes." She wraps a leg around my back, seating me deeper inside. "Don't pull out. I want all of you."

My hips unleash, pounding into her over and over. A growl shreds my throat as I finally spill myself inside her, marking her like I've never marked another.

I bury my face in her neck as I try to comprehend what the hell she's doing to me, to understand the feelings she evokes, but when it comes to this woman in my arms, sometimes there is no understanding. Only feeling.

CHAPTER NINE

Zoey

The moon begins to make its appearance, a million stars hovering above us as I lie draped across Austin's chest in the bed of his truck, the steady rhythm of his heart beating beneath my cheek. His fingers dance along my back while mine sweep across his hard stomach.

Silence graces us, nothing but the sound of Mother Nature whispering in the distance. For the first time in months, everything in my world feels right and it only thickens the guilt I harbor inside.

"You're right. I'm scared," I whisper into the dark, admitting a truth I haven't been able to face. One he deserves to hear.

His fingers still, waiting for what I will say next.

"I've lost everyone who was supposed to love me and every day I fight to not lose my sister, too. The thought of taking this and eventually losing you…it scares me to death."

Silence hangs thick, my anxious heart fearing I've messed this up too much this time and he won't forgive me, despite what just happened between us.

"You're scared I'm going to leave you, and I'm fucking terrified that I'll never be able to."

My eyes close in regret, the magnitude of what that means bearing down on me.

"Yet here we are. Somehow always ending up right where we're meant to be."

The truth settles around my heart like a warm fire. He rolls me to my back, situating himself between my open thighs. His face hangs inches from mine, his usual patient eyes burning in frustration.

"I don't want to be your friend anymore, Zoey. I've tried, really fucking tried, but I want more. I want this right here." His thumb strokes my cheek, gentle and soothing just like the man himself.

"I do too," I admit softly, my fingers circling his wrist as I lean into his touch. "I really am sorry about yesterday. I wasn't upset with you. I wasn't even upset you were there to see her. She loved it. She loves you…"

My words trail off as I think about how disappointed Chrissy was when I walked back into her room without him. It made me feel even worse.

"I had a run-in with my mother," I tell him, anger thickening my throat. "She came to see me at the bar."

His curious eyes search mine. "What did she want?"

"Money," I answer, practically spitting the word. "She didn't even bother to ask about Chrissy or even me for that matter. All she cared about was herself and supporting her habit."

"Did you tell her to fuck off?" His voice is tight, laced with anger.

"Not in those exact words but yeah, I did. Then she said we were the worst mistakes of her life," the admission falls on a sad whisper. I hate myself for it. Hate that I even let her evoke that emotion from me anymore.

He rests his forehead on mine, his warm gaze penetrating soul deep. "Well you're the best mistake of mine."

My heart dances to a new beat, the beautiful words proving it's not broken beyond repair. "A mistake?" I ask, quirking a brow.

"You tell me. Are you going to keep pushing me away, denying what we both want?"

The answer I want to give dangles in the back of my throat, and he senses my hesitation.

"Talk to me, Zoey. For once, just lay it all out."

I think about a disease that has not only affected my sister's life but mine, too. "I never thought my life would be like this. I had so many plans to live out my dream as a photographer, to get away from my parents' toxic relationship. I was going to leave town and never look back. Then Chrissy was born and the opposite happened. I don't regret it, not even for a second. But some days are hard, really hard, and I'm so tired," I confess, feeling guilty for the admission.

"It's okay to be tired, Zoey. It's a lot for one person to take on, but you don't have to do it alone. I'm right here, willing to take it with you. You just have to let me."

My hand moves to the side of his face, fingers fanning his jaw as I gaze back into his warm eyes. "I don't deserve you."

"You're wrong. *You* deserve this. You deserve to be happy."

Swallowing thickly, I tell him what I struggle with most. "Every day I walk into that hospital and always wonder, why her and not me? It's not fair."

"You're right, it's not, but her disease is not your fault. You have to stop punishing yourself. There's a reason you're here with me and I'm selfishly thankful for that."

I have to wonder if he's right. Maybe he's *my* reason just as much as I'm Chrissy's reason…

Deep, dark eyes that are filled with patience and understanding peer down at me as he brushes a piece of hair from my face. "Let me in, Zoey. Let me love you the way you deserve."

Love, it can be meant in so many different ways. I know that if I let this man in that the love between us could be the one that never dies. It's terrifying yet tempting all at once. An offer I can no longer refuse because I also know he will love my sister too, and if anyone deserves more love, it's her.

"You're impossible to turn down, Hawke. You know that?"

"Is that a yes?"

I wrap my arms around his neck, a soft smile teasing my lips. "That's a yes."

His mouth splits into a sexy smirk. "About fucking time."

A giggle escapes me that is effectively cut off by his mouth. He kisses me slow and deep, his tongue parting my lips and sliding inside to do an erotic dance.

I drown in his essence, my heart and body soaring for more. With more confidence than I feel, I push him to his back and crawl over top of him, my knees straddling his hips. Reaching down, I grab the material at my waist and pull my sundress over my head, unveiling more than just my body, but all of me.

Every broken, damaged piece.

His sharp inhale penetrates the air as his eyes turn to liquid fire. "All fucking mine," he growls, reaching up to palm my breasts. "Tell me, baby. Tell me you're mine."

"I'm yours."

They are suddenly the easiest words I've ever said.

"Show me."

Biting my lip, I grab his hard cock between us and slide down on it. Our moans mingle in the heated night air. My hands brace on his hard stomach as I rock my hips, taking him deep.

"That's it, Zoey girl. Ride me hard." He sits up, banning an arm around my back as his lips press to the base of my throat, traveling their way down before latching onto a hard, pink nipple.

Pleasure dances along my skin, the stars above me blurring as I drop my head back and become lost in the perfect world he and I create.

For the rest of the night, we lose ourselves in each other. Hands and lips, heated touches and desires. We make passionate love until the morning sun wakes us then we do it all over again as I finally let this man have all of me.

CHAPTER TEN

Austin

The residential street is calm and quiet as I pull up to Jake's house, parking directly behind Cam's truck. The text came in an hour ago, telling us to meet him here before work.

It was hard to pull myself away from the warm body I woke up next to, a woman who I've been lucky enough to share a few nights with this past week. If Zoey isn't in my bed then I'm seeing her at the bar before shifts or at the hospital after a long day, which is even better because then I get to see Chrissy, too. Another girl who has come to mean a lot to me.

I've completely lost my fucking mind over both of them and it's the best feeling in the world. Especially when I no longer have to convince Zoey of it. Ever since that afternoon at my house, it's like a switch went off, something I said or did finally made her trust me. It's a trust I vow to never break.

Climbing the front steps, I raise my fist to knock only to have the door swing open and a pissed-off teenager come barreling out of it, slamming right into my chest.

"Whoa." I grab onto a pair of slender shoulders that are cloaked in black just like the rest of her body.

"Shit," Charlie curses under her breath. Steel blue eyes peer up at me beneath dark lashes, her long pink cotton candy colored hair shielding half her face.

Must be the color of the day. The girl changes her hair as much as I do my underwear. "Hey, half pint, what's your hurry?"

Annoyance sparks in her eyes, mingling with the pain that always lurks there. It's been there since the fire that took the lives of her parents and left her scarred for the rest of her life. Which is exactly why she is covered from head to toe, despite the warm day.

"Oh good, you're here." Her sarcasm runs thick, contradicting the greeting. "Maybe you can talk some sense into my asshole brother since the other one can't." She darts a glare over her shoulder to where Cam and Jake are standing in the kitchen.

Jake's arms are crossed over his chest, a pissed-off expression on his face while Cam looks thoroughly amused.

Without another word, she hefts her backpack further up her shoulder and slips past me.

I quirk a brow at my two best friends. "Looks like it's been a good morning."

"I swear that girl lives to torture me," Jake growls.

"What happened now?" I step inside, closing the door behind me.

"She had a fucking guy over here yesterday while I was at work."

Well that explains why he's so pissed off. Can't say I blame him. Though, I have to admit I'm surprised she had anyone over, let alone a guy. Since her parents' death, Charlie has pretty much kept to herself. We never see her with any friends because she's usually hiding herself from the world.

"She says they're just friends," Cam explains, sensing where my thoughts are.

"Maybe they are."

"It doesn't matter," Jake snaps. "She knows the rules. Not only do I have that damn school calling me every other week, but now I have to worry about her bringing guys over here. I did not sign up for this shit!" Amongst his frustration is guilt. He drops into the kitchen chair, defeated. "I'm royally fucking this up."

Cam claps him on the shoulder. "Come on, man. She's a teenager. We got into way more shit when we were her age. This is typical stuff."

This is true. If she started doing half the shit we did at her age then

I would be concerned.

Jake doesn't seem as convinced. "The school suggested some counseling sessions. Maybe they're right."

"It can't hurt," I say, taking a spot at the table. "Maybe that's what she needs. Someone to talk to."

"She can talk to me, damn it," he counters.

I feel like telling him that he is not the easiest person to talk to, especially when the two of them are constantly biting each other's heads off. However, I decide now is not the best time to bring that up.

"Whatever. Let's drop it. This isn't why I asked you guys over here." He sits back in his chair, expression grim. "I spoke to Ted Hamilton from arson yesterday. I wanted the answers Roper isn't giving us and he asked me to go for a drive with him to the apartment building, or rather, what's left of it."

"Let me guess, he tried pulling you over to their side," Cam says, annoyance thick in his voice.

Unlike Roper, Ted Hamilton was good friends with Jake's father. He's been an arson investigator for almost thirty years. The moment Jake graduated from the academy, Hamilton has tried recruiting him over to their department. Much to Roper's dismay.

Jake nods. "He did and my answer was the same as always."

I'm actually surprised Jake doesn't consider it more. He's always had a knack for figuring out fires, learning them, studying them, something he inherited from his father. But more recently, I think it stems from him trying to figure out how a fire bested his father.

Dale Ryan was one of the finest firemen in Colorado before becoming a lead investigator. He was a good man, someone we all looked up to.

Jake has that same intuition his father did. Even Cap has brought him in before asking his thoughts on certain situations for a report. He would make a damn fine investigator just like his father, but I know he loves being front and center like Cam and me, fighting the lethal flames head-on.

I'm selfishly glad he has chosen to stay on my squad. All of us made a pact long ago. We stick together, always. We've been that way since we were kids. All of us finding each other at our first hockey practice when we were only five years old. Jase was part of that pact until he transferred to South Carolina for Sam, something I can't fault him for because I know without a doubt I would move across the fucking world for Zoey, let alone the country.

"I did end up going with him though," Jake continues. "Mainly because I want information, more than what we're getting from Roper. This bastard has struck twice now, both times on our watch. I want answers."

"Did he tell you anything?" I ask.

"Not as much as I hoped. They're scrambling for answers themselves and overloaded with cases right now. But he did tell me some of the chemicals that have been used." He pauses, expression tightening further. "The mixture this asshole is using is more than lethal, it's unheard of. Nothing like any MO they have encountered before."

"How so?"

"Usually in arson situations, the arsonist wants you to know it's been set intentionally. They like to display power but this guy has been good at leading them in different directions. That's why they originally thought the warehouse fire was electrical. It was staged that way. It was also strategically set for them to figure out it wasn't but not until he was ready."

"He's playing games," Cam remarks, anger edging his voice.

Jake nods.

"So what did you find at the apartment?" I ask.

"Not much. It wasn't until I was home that I made an interesting discovery."

Jake grabs a folder that rests on the kitchen table, flipping it open. He pulls out blueprints of the apartment building. Red marker runs through it in every direction. It's clear he's studied it for hours.

"This is originally where they thought the fire started," he says, pointing to the ground floor. "Set behind the walls which would make sense with how it travelled so fast, but when I took a closer look at the wires, something was off. The burn pattern didn't match up with the others."

"So you don't think it was started from the ground floor?" I ask, trying to understand where he's going with this.

"Actually, I do, but I also believe it was started in two other locations at the exact same time."

Cam's eyes pull up. "How is that possible?"

"With this." Jake pulls out a sheet of paper, an image of a small device that can only be described as a bomb.

"Explosives?" Cam says, sounding as doubtful as I feel.

"Yeah."

"Roper didn't mention anything about explosives," I remind him. "Evidence would be left behind."

"Not this one. This particular bomb is made to disintegrate upon explosion, leaving no evidence behind but one thing…"

"What's that?" I ask when he trails off.

"A distinctive odor. Sweet and musky."

Realization hits me like a ton of bricks, the knowledge burning in my mind and heart.

"Well holy shit," Cam says, sitting back. "Einstein here figured it out."

Jake grunts. "I haven't figured out shit, not yet anyway, but I'm working on it. This can only be detonated by a push of a button, which means this asshole was watching, waiting for the right time to set it off."

"Did you tell Hamilton?" I ask.

"Yeah. He's going to take it to Roper but whoever is doing this isn't just some pyro off the street Googling this shit. This is someone who knows a thing or two about fires, reactors, and chemicals."

"You think it could be one of our own?" Cam asks, a heaviness falling with that suggestion.

"I think there's too many unanswered questions to go that route yet, but I say we rule nothing out. Whoever this is, is smart, really smart, and if they don't catch him quick his destruction will only escalate."

No doubt it fears us most. We already lost Declan, almost lost a little boy. If we don't catch this motherfucker soon, then who will be next?

CHAPTER ELEVEN

Zoey

I sit next to my sister's bed, her hand gently clasped in mine as she watches one of her favorite TV shows with Gus cuddled in beside her. Her eyes are riveted on the screen while mine are taking in how weak and tired she looks. I left work early when I heard she was having a rough day.

It started at breakfast when she wasn't strong enough to hold her spoon. Then her juice didn't go down well, spilling all over her. As the day went on she only became more agitated, even lashing out at Dina. She has since refused to eat dinner, defeat beating down her newfound spirit.

My heart hurts that she's had a setback but I also understand her frustration. She was making strides and to be thrown back to square one in a single day is hard. She has calmed down since I showed up and seems more well rested which is most important.

"Are you hungry yet?" I ask, wishing she would eat something. She needs her nutrition, especially right now.

She barely shakes her head, her eyes remaining on the TV.

A knock on the door has both of us looking over. My heart leaps at the man standing in the doorway, a sexy grin resting on his handsome face. Dressed in fire gear, he holds two bouquets of flowers.

"A-Au-sdin," Chrissy greets him before I can, a spark of enthusiasm entering her voice for the first time since I've been here today.

"What are you doing here?" I ask, climbing to my feet. As far as I knew he was still supposed to be on shift for a few more hours.

"I've come bearing gifts." He hands me a bouquet of daffodils, dropping a kiss on my cheek that leaves my skin tingling before moving to my sister, kneeling before her to do the same, only her bouquet is lilies. "Your sister told me pink is your favorite color."

"Y-yes. Th-Th-..." Her eyes close in frustration.

"You're welcome," he says, forcing her not to finish. "Tomorrow will be better, kid. I know it." His inspiring words have emotion burning my throat.

I texted him earlier to tell him she was having a bad day and that I would be staying the night with her. Not only was he understanding but now he shows up here with this sweet gesture. Right when I didn't think I could fall any more in love with him, I'm proven wrong.

After a soft kiss to her hand and a pat to Gus's head, Austin stands to his feet, facing me. "I can't stay long. I have some of the guys waiting outside in the truck. We were just making a run to the grocery store and I wanted to drop by and see my favorite girls."

The most beautiful feeling skips its way into my heart. Chrissy and I have never belonged to anyone and it feels good to belong to this man.

"F-F-ire tr-uck?" Chrissy manages.

Austin turns back to her. "Yeah, we always make runs with it while on shift. You wanna come and see?" His eyes swing to mine. "If it's okay?"

I nod before looking over at Chrissy. "What do you say? Want to go see it?"

She doesn't have to speak, the answer is written all over her excited face.

"One second. I'll get your chair." I head out into the hallway to grab her wheelchair, then let Dina know that we will be back in a few minutes.

When I enter the room again, Austin is already lifting her out of bed. He easily places her into the chair and even straps her in, remembering from the last time. He makes sure to place Gus on her lap then he takes it upon himself to be the one to wheel her out of the room and into the elevator. He looks so at ease, so right. The same way he fits in every other part of my life.

I send him an appreciative smile, loving how he just turned around our whole day. He flashes me a wink along with that killer smirk that makes me weak in the knees. It has me remembering every dirty thing he has done to me this past week. Things I had no idea my body was even capable of feeling...until him.

Parked right outside the front doors is the massive fire truck, a few of the guys sitting inside. Chrissy's eyes light up, her entire face beaming at the sight.

"Hey," Cam announces, jumping out of the truck with that charming grin of his, Jake trailing not far behind.

"You came back with beautiful women, you sly devil," he says to Austin before laying a smacking kiss on my cheek. It earns him a glare from the man next to me but he pays it no mind, moving to kneel before my sister. "What's your name, beautiful?"

"This is my sister, Chrissy," I tell him, saving her from having to speak.

"Nice to meet you, Chrissy. I'm Cam, the best looking firefighter in the state of Colorado."

A choppy laugh leaves my sister, a blush staining her cheeks. Leave it to Cam to have Chrissy swooning all over the place.

"This guy behind me is Jake. He's the grouchy one."

Jake grunts but offers my sister a smile. "How's it going, Chrissy?" His head turns my way next, giving a small nod. "Zoey."

"Hey, Jake."

"That's Carl," Austin says, pointing to the one sitting in the driver's seat.

I give him a wave and receive a nod in return.

"You ever see a fire truck before?" Cam asks my sister.

"N-No."

"Come on then. Allow me to introduce you to the beast." Cam elbows Austin out of the way and pushes her chair closer.

"Be careful with her," Austin warns, a protectiveness in his tone that warms my heart. He turns my way, catching me watching him. "What's going on in that pretty head of yours, Zoey girl?"

My fingers curl in his shirt to pull him down and he doesn't hesitate giving me what I silently seek. His lips land on mine, the simple touch skipping its way through my entire body.

When my tongue flicks his lip, a low growl leaves his throat, his arm banding around my back as he deepens the kiss. I wind my arms around his neck, moaning when I feel his erection at my belly.

By the time he pulls back, I'm breathless, my mind lost in a state of euphoria that only this man can bring me. "You just made a bad day beautiful. Thank you," I whisper, wishing he understood just how much this means to Chrissy and me.

His expression sobers, concern flashing in his eyes. "How is she?"

I shrug. "She'll be okay. Just a hard day. I think she's more frustrated than anything."

"And how about you, Zoey? How are you doing?"

The question is so foreign to me that it actually takes me a moment to answer. I'm not used to having someone think of me during the hard times.

"A whole lot better now thanks to you," I answer honestly.

"Good." His arms hug me closer, providing me a warmth only he can. "What do you have going on tomorrow afternoon?"

"Depends."

"On?"

"On whatever you're about to say."

Amusement flickers across his face. "I want you to come pick out a swing for my porch."

"Really?" I ask, excited at the prospect. I've been telling him all week that his porch is what dreams are made of and he needs one.

"Yes, *really*. Whichever one you want, it's yours. Then I want to fuck you on it."

A laugh explodes past my lips at the blunt remark. "You are so sweet."

"You know it. So what do you say?"

"As long as Chrissy is doing okay then I would love to. I don't have to be at the bar until four."

"Then it's tentatively booked. If you need to be here though with Chrissy we can reschedule. No problem."

Understanding and patience. It's all I ever get from him. Sometimes I wonder how I thought this would never work. Now I can't picture my life without him.

"You're making me fall hard and fast, Austin Hawke."

"Good. Because I've been waiting all along, ready to catch you."

The beautiful words light up every sad and lonely place inside of me.

"Kiss me again," I demand, rising to the tips of my toes.

"My fucking pleasure." The words leave him on another growl as he meets me halfway, taking my mouth in a searing kiss that sends my senses reeling.

"Hey, you two! Don't make me pull the hose out," Cam bellows, pulling us apart.

Biting back a smile, I glance over Austin's shoulder to find him standing next to my giggling sister, looking rather impressed with himself.

Austin, however, isn't the least bit amused. "That guy really gets on my fucking nerves sometimes," he grumbles.

"Come on, he's not so bad. Besides, he's your best friend."

He grunts. "Yeah, my annoying best friend who needs to learn to keep his lips off my woman."

My brow lifts. "Jealous, Hawke?"

His expression darkens, making my pulse kick-start. "You know better than that, Zoey. We both know who you belong to, and if we weren't surrounded by people right now, I'd gladly remind you."

The possessive words set my body ablaze, building a raging inferno between my legs. His lips kick up in a grin, knowing the effect he has on me.

Just then, his radio comes to life, breaking up our moment.

"Fire Station Two, we have a vehicle collision on the bridge, one victim trapped and several others injured."

"Bring it in!" Austin orders, all of them moving quickly. He drops a brief kiss to my lips and takes enough time to drop one on my sister's cheek before he jumps into the passenger seat.

Cam hangs out the window as the truck roars to life, its sirens wailing through the air. "Nice to meet you, Chrissy. See you soon, Zoey."

"Be careful!" I yell out just as the truck pulls away, but I don't miss the parting wink Austin shoots me. It has butterflies flocking in my tummy.

The fire truck gets lost in the distance, taking the man who owns my heart with it. When the sirens are barely a muffled cry, I take Chrissy up to her room and have an orderly help get her back in bed.

I take the spot next to her again, loving how much more relaxed and at ease she looks. "The fire truck was pretty cool, wasn't it?"

She doesn't answer and gazes back at me in a way she never has before, something soft reflecting in her eyes. Her trembling hand struggles to lift to my cheek.

I lean in closer, making it easier for her. "What?" I ask, my hand covering hers as I hold it close.

"D-D-oey h-h-appy."

"Of course. I'm always happy when I'm with you, silly."

"N-o. A-Aus-din."

My heart pinches in my chest. "He makes me happy too but you are always first, Chrissy. You know that, right?"

She closes her eyes briefly and when she reopens them there are tears glistening in their depths. "Not fa-ir."

"Yes, it is," I tell her firmly, knowing where her head is at. "We're a team, you and me, remember? I wouldn't have it any other way. Okay?"

She nods but the assurance doesn't quite reach her eyes.

"How about a story before bed?" I reach down at the small bookshelf next to her bed, pulling out the few books she has. "Which one?"

Her eyes land on the same one she always chooses. *A Kiss From Heaven: An Animal's Love Beyond.*

"How did I know?" I say, giving her a teasing smile.

She returns it. "M-My fav-orite."

"Mine too."

It's a beautiful book that every child who has lost a pet should read. It's about how animals find the same love and peace people do. The message of the book is that every time a rainbow appears it's a kiss from heaven.

Chrissy's head is rested back, eyes softly closed as she absorbs every bit of the story, a sweet smile on her face.

Once I finish, her eyes open, questions burning in her gaze. "Sa-ame f-or pe-ople?"

"Yes, it's the same for people."

"Th-at's wh-ere I'll go?"

Agony seizes my chest. "One day, Chrissy, we will all go there but not for a very long time."

The uncertainty reflecting back at me absolutely breaks my heart.

"Listen to me. We are going to get through this. It won't be this hard all the time. We will find what works for you and then you will come live with me. I'll give you the life I promised. Okay?"

She nods shakily. "Lo-ove you."

"I love you, too."

I crawl in next to her, needing to hold her more than ever. It isn't long before she falls asleep, curled into my chest. I meant every word I said. I will get her through this. I will get us the life I've always promised if it's the last thing I do.

CHAPTER TWELVE

Austin

"A little higher." Zoey stands a few feet away as I hang the porch swing she picked out earlier today, the sun casting a glow as if each ray shines only for her.

She's dressed in cutoff jean shorts that have been tempting me all day, leaving her long legs on display. Legs I love to feel wrapped around my waist as I'm driving myself into her tight, warm body. The snug light blue tank top she wears matches her eyes and molds to her chest like…

The knowing smile she flashes my way snaps me from the thought. "I said higher," she reminds me, barely containing a laugh.

"Sorry, I got distracted."

"Clearly." Amusement edges her tone, the soft sound of her voice infiltrating my chest, like always.

I'm so fucked over this woman.

I lift the front chain higher, looking back at her for approval. Once I'm granted it, I screw it in then do the same with the back one. Just as I start in on the very last chain, she appears before me, slipping her hand beneath my shirt and raking her nails gently down my stomach.

My cock jumps, a growl leaving my throat. "Zoey." Her name falls with warning as the screw slips from my fingers before I catch it.

"Yes?" she asks, nothing but sweet innocence coating her tone.

"Let me finish this first."

"How about you finish and I start." No sooner than the remark leaves her does she drop to her knees before me, working on my belt.

My jaw locks, muscles flexing as I practically screw a hole right through my fucking roof. She releases my stiff cock into her hand, stroking me from base to tip.

"Fuck it!" I just finish the last bolt before throwing my drill over the railing and onto the lawn.

Laughter dominates her expression as her hand continues to torture me. After ridding myself of my shirt, my fingers drive through her hair, tilting her face up to mine. "Suck it, Zoey. Put it in your mouth."

A spark of heat ignites in her eyes. "Yes, sir, Lieutenant." She leans forward, taking me into the heat of her mouth.

My mind spins with lust, need pushing its way up my spine as she takes me all the way to her throat.

"That's it, Zoey girl," I groan. "Just like that."

Her lashes sweep up, eyes hooded with desire as she renews her efforts.

"Such a dirty girl. You like my cock in your mouth, baby?"

She hums her response, sucking her way back to the top to give me a show, her pink tongue swirling the tip.

It drives me fucking wild. Growling, I thrust forward once, testing her boundaries.

She shifts onto her knees, relaxing her jaw as she gives me full control.

I take it as a sign and begin fucking her mouth with deep strokes, my hips relentless. Fire spreads through my veins, hurtling me closer to destruction, but I manage to hold off just at the last second, needing to be inside of her when she takes me over the edge.

"Not yet." I pull out and lift her to her feet, my mouth descending on hers with greed.

Her need collides with my own, our tongues lashing in a blaze of fury, stoking the fire that always burns between us.

Her shirt leaves her next, then her bra. I turn her around, pulling her back against me as I cup the heavy weight of her tits, flicking her tight little nipples.

She drops her head on my chest, her ass cradling my cock as she pushes back for more.

"You wet, Zoey girl?" I ask, my lips grazing her ear.

"Yes." The confession is nothing but a breathless whisper.

"Show me," I order, voice dark. "Stick your hand in your panties and let me taste."

Her hand disappears into her shorts for a few glorious seconds before she brings a single finger to my mouth.

The sweet taste of her explodes on my tongue and the little control I was clinging to snaps. I walk us forward a few steps, stopping just before the railing. Shoving her shorts and panties down her long legs, I lift her right knee to rest on the banister, her slick pussy ready for the taking.

"Hold on, baby. This is going to be a hard fuck." It's the only warning she gets before I drive in deep, filling every inch of her.

Her heated cry shatters the air, mingling with the summer heat and seeping into my hot blood. She grips the railing as I hammer into her, chasing a need I can't explain. Every pent-up emotion I have when it comes to her pours out of me, making me feel like a fucking animal with every savage thrust.

"Goddamn, Zoey, we're good together," I groan, watching my cock disappear in and out of her.

"It's always so good," she moans.

"You know what the best part is?"

"What?" she breathes.

"You're all fucking mine." Leaning down, I press a kiss to her damp shoulder then cheek, my lips cherishing her while my cock destroys her.

She curls an arm around my neck and turns her face, lips meeting mine in a kiss of possession that rivals my own.

Straightening, my hands grip her hips, digging into the supple flesh as I ride her harder and faster.

"Austin, I can't hold off any longer." It's the only warning I get before her body trembles with release, and the whimpers that fall from her mouth have me coming right behind her, my thrusts never faltering until we're both spent.

It takes several long moments before we both catch our breaths. Once we're able to grasp some form of reality, I pull out and the disconnection is hollowing. If I could live inside this woman every day for the rest of my life, I would.

While I pull my pants up she throws on my plaid button-down I had on earlier, the material engulfing her body. The sight of her wearing my clothes will be ingrained into my memory forever.

A shy smile eases across her lips when she catches me watching her. "I like it when you look at me like that, Hawke. It makes me feel beautiful."

She has no idea how beautiful she is. No idea the things I want to do to her, the future I want with her.

"Come here, Zoey." Taking her hand, I pull her down on the swing with me, gathering her into my arms.

She curls into my chest with a contented sigh, the swing long enough to accommodate our stretched-out bodies. "Thank you for asking me to do this with you today. It's exactly what I needed."

"You don't have to thank me, Zoey. I always want you with me."

I feel her smile against my chest, but despite the easy moment, I sense her mind a million miles away.

"Are you going to tell me what's bothering you or are you going to make me guess?"

She lifts her chin, peeking up at me. "Can never pull one over on you, can I?"

"Never. Now what's wrong?"

She shrugs. "Just thinking about Chrissy."

"I thought you said she was better this morning?"

"She was. Or seemed to be. The doctor is hopeful with the new medication and so am I but...she's been acting different lately. More defeated, more...hopeless..." She trails off, shaking her head. "I don't know. I can't explain it. Something is off and I just feel so helpless. I wish I could have her live with me but I just don't have the means to do that yet."

"You know I'll help you, right? Anything you need, Zoey. Money included."

She tilts her face up to mine, expression softening. "I know you would and I appreciate that, but this financial burden isn't your responsibility."

"It's ours. You and me. Remember?"

"Yes, but not financially. Not this, Austin. I appreciate your support but I cannot accept your money. Please understand that."

As frustrated as it makes me, I expected it. She has too much damn pride. The truth is, though, I've already been taking steps, looking into ways I can make my place wheelchair accessible, because if I have my way, both of them will be living with me eventually. I'm just going to have to tread carefully. Take it slow.

"All right, then how about we bring her out here for an afternoon?" I suggest. "We can have a barbecue and take her down by the creek."

She straightens, pushing up on her hands to look at me. "Really?"

"Why not? Maybe that's what she needs, to get out and see something other than the hospital."

She bites her lip, contemplating the idea. "I've always wanted to take her out on my own but I've been nervous in case she has a seizure, but she hasn't had one in weeks."

"Even then, I'm a first responder. If anything were to happen I can help her, but I'm sure it won't come to that. We'll have her come for a few hours. See how she does."

I watch the wheels turn in her head and know the exact moment she accepts the idea. She throws her arms around my neck, hugging me tight. "Thank you," she whispers. "Thank you for always thinking of her, for thinking of us both."

"I'd do anything for you and Chrissy. You have to know that by now."

She pulls back, her hand moving to my jaw. "I do and it means so much to me. I can't wait for her to see your place. She'll love it like I do."

Little does she know, this is her place, too. She left her mark on it that night months ago.

"We should make it a housewarming party?" she says.

My brow cocks at the idea. "A party?"

"Yeah, just something small. Chrissy has never been to anything like that."

I shrug. "If that's what you want. I can invite a few of the guys from the squad." I pause, treading carefully with what I say next. "I can invite my parents, too, if you want."

A sweet smile takes over her face. "You want me to meet your parents, Hawke?"

"Damn right, and I want my mom to tell you all the reasons why I'm the perfect guy. She kinda loves me, a lot."

She releases one of her giggles but it fades quickly. "She doesn't need to tell me how amazing you are. I already know." Leaning in, her lips gently brush mine.

I cup the back of her neck and deepen it, needing more.

Always more.

Within minutes, she takes me inside her body again, my favorite place to be. No more words are spoken but none need to be. She knows where I stand, what I want, and I have no doubt she wants it, too.

One day I will make it happen. I'll give her everything she's ever wanted. Now that I have her, I'm never letting go.

CHAPTER THIRTEEN

Zoey

Laughter fills the yard, the smell of barbecue lingering in the air as Cam, Jake, and Austin, among a few others from the fire station, play football with my sister.

I stand on the sidelines with a smile, watching the game unfold. I worried when Chrissy woke up this morning feeling tired and sluggish that this get-together would be too much for her but today could not have gone better. Her eyes may be tired but her smile is as radiant as mine. I don't think I have ever seen her this happy.

Before everyone arrived it was just the three of us and we took her down by the creek. It's probably my favorite place on the property. It was a bit of a struggle with her chair so Austin carried her the entire time, holding her weak body in his strong arms. It's a memory that will stay with me forever.

We kept the gathering fairly small with only Austin's closest friends, his rescue squad, including his captain, and also his parents, who have turned out to be some of the loveliest people I've ever met. Even Frank came by to meet her before going to the bar. Everyone welcomed us with open arms and went out of their way to make my sister feel special.

Today I've witnessed what family truly means in every sense of the word. Not only by Austin's interactions with his parents but also his squad. Austin's relationship with Jake and Cam has always been close but this afternoon I've realized it's so much more than that. They are no doubt a band of brothers who would do anything for the other, their bond running deeper than friendship.

"Watch where you throw that damn thing," Captain Gypsy shouts, dodging the football that Jake just threw at him.

By the smirk Jake gives, it's clear it was intentional.

"I thought you were supposed to be an All State quarterback, Ryan?"

The entire squad laughs at the dig, Cam being the loudest one of all.

"I can out throw you any day, old man," Jake tosses back.

"Old man?" The captain returns, clearly offended. "I'll show you what this 'old man' can do." He drops his half eaten burger and strides to the field, ready for battle.

The captain's attitude may be surly but it's obvious how much he cares for his team and it's clear the men respect him a lot.

Cam gets into position and when the captain makes the call, he snaps it. Austin quickly intercepts, dropping the ball in my sister's lap.

Chrissy laughs as Cam dramatically dodges out of the way of her chair, landing on his back while Austin races across the end zone with her.

"Touch down!" He raises my sister's arm in the air, showcasing her victory, and it has the biggest smile taking over her face.

"Yay, Chrissy!" I applaud loudly.

Austin's eyes meet mine, flashing me a wink that sends a flutter through my belly. It doesn't help that he's shirtless, all those glorious abs on display, damp with sweat.

That signature smirk spreads across his lips as he senses exactly where my thoughts are.

"My son is smitten."

I turn at the soft female voice and find Laurel Hawke coming to stand next to me, a kind smile on her face as she watches the game. The woman is not only kind but beautiful as well. Her skin tone is warm, hair short and light brown. She also has the same kind brown eyes as Austin.

"You think so?" I ask, unable to deny the hope that comment instills.

"I know so. I've never seen him look at a woman like he does you."

"Well, that means a lot coming from you," I tell her. "I care very deeply for him. You've raised a great man. He's done a lot for my sister and me."

Her gaze meets mine, pride etched on her face. "My son takes care of the people he loves. He's strong and honorable. Qualities he gets from his father."

Austin may share those qualities with his father but he no doubt gets his generous heart from his mother. She has gone out of her way today to be kind to me and to get to know my sister.

"Listen, honey, Austin has told me a little bit about you and your sister. Now I don't mean to overstep but I want you to know that even though we have only just met if you ever need anything, anything at all, I'm just a phone call away."

"Thank you." My voice is barely a whisper as I fight to keep my emotions at bay. "I appreciate that."

Her hand lifts, touching my shoulder. "If you're important to my son, you are important to me."

She and my mother are like night and day. It makes me wonder how different my and Chrissy's life would have been if we had someone who cared for us the way she cares for her son.

Our conversation ceases when Austin's father, Jack, walks over to join us, linking arms with his wife. "What are you two beautiful ladies talking about over here?"

"How amazing our son is," she tells him honestly, unconditional love thick in her voice.

His gaze shifts to mine. "He's a good boy. Gets his good looks from me." He flashes me the same playful wink his son just did minutes ago.

Laurel slaps his arm. "You're incorrigible, Jack Hawke," she scolds, but can't hide her smile.

All of it makes me smile, though I must admit. Austin is the spitting image of his father.

He wraps an arm around her shoulder, pulling her in close. "How about you and me go for a walk on the trails? Take in some scenery." The suggestive look he shoots her puts a slight blush on her face.

"Well, how can I refuse that?" She turns my way. "Excuse us, dear."

"Of course. Have fun."

They walk across the yard, hand in hand, heading in the direction of the creek. Seeing their love for one another is foreign to me. I never had it growing up. Until a short time ago, I never thought it existed. Now I realize just how wrong I've been.

"Zoey," Austin calls my attention from across the yard. "Get out here."

I raise my hands out in front of me, the thought terrifying. "No, that's okay. I'm good with just watching."

"Come on," he coaxes. "Come play." That lazy grin I love so much eases on his face, wearing down my resolve.

"Yeah, come play with us," Cam chimes in. "You can be on my team and we can kick your boyfriend's ass together."

A laugh tumbles past my lips at the glare Austin sends him.

"Forget it, asshole. She's on my team. Get your own damn girl-friend."

"But yours is so hot."

Austin shoves him, hard enough to make him stumble before he jogs across the yard, extending his hand to me. "Come on, Zoey girl. Don't make me throw you over my shoulder."

"I don't know the first thing about football. I'll make a complete fool out of myself."

"You're too pretty to be a fool."

His sweet words settle around my heart like a warm blanket. Regardless of the compliment, I keep my feet firmly planted and shake my head.

"Fine. You leave me no choice." He ducks, lunging forward, and throws me over his shoulder, just like he said he would.

A bunch of whistles and catcalls are made by the guys while my sister's stuttering laugh travels above it all.

"You're crazy, put me down right now." The threat is weak at best because I can't deny how great my view is right now, watching every muscle in his back flex as he strides across the yard is no hard feat.

After a playful smack to my bottom, he finally places me on my feet. I blow a strand of hair out of my face, my hands planting on my hips as I take in his proud stance. "Just for that, Hawke. I'm switching teams."

My feet retract as I start backing up toward Cam. His eyes darken in warning, the narrow slits sending a flutter to ripple through me.

Cam is more than amused and eagerly awaits me with open arms but just at the last minute, I move in next to the captain, causing them all to break into hysterics, even triggering a smirk from Austin.

Cam grabs his chest in mock pain. "Zoey, babe, that cut me deep."

The captain throws an arm over my shoulder. "That's because she's smart and knows a winner when she sees one."

"Can you believe this, Chrissy?" Austin says to my sister, arms crossed over his bare chest. "She traded us in."

"I-It's o-n." She tosses back playfully.

"Bring it, sis."

Jake calls us in to a huddle and gives the rundown of the play; all of it sounding like a bunch of gibberish to me. Afterward, the captain leads me to my position on the field then proceeds to tell me our plan of attack.

The entire time I listen, I can feel Austin's eyes on me, the promise of retribution to come. It sends heat spiraling down to my toes.

When Jake calls for the ball and Cam snaps it to him, I run across the field to where the captain instructed me. Just as Jake makes the pass, I jump in front of Cam, and to my surprise, I catch it.

I gasp in excitement, staring down at my hands in disbelief. "Oh my god, I caught it."

"Run for your life, kid!" the captain bellows, waving his arms wildly in the other direction.

Looking up, I see everyone coming straight for me. With a shriek, I bolt as fast as I can toward the end zone, my tennis shoes slipping on the soft grass.

"I got her!"

One final glance behind me and I find Austin hot on my heels while the others hang back, watching in amusement. I push myself harder and make the touchdown just before his arms circle my waist. He takes us to the ground, his strong body bracing our fall.

I laugh as he rolls me beneath him, his playful expression hovering above me. "You can run, Zoey girl, but I'll always catch you."

My heart prances in my chest. "Is that a promise?"

"Damn straight." His mouth lands on mine with a growl, claiming my heart along with my lips.

The ball falls away, my arms wrapping around his neck as I become lost in all the beautiful feelings he evokes within me.

"Well look at that," Cam's boisterous voice breaks up our moment. "Looks like Hawke finally knows what it's like to score in the end zone."

Another round of laughs explode through the air, including mine.

"I'm so going to kick his ass," he grumbles before pushing off the ground to stand, his hand reaching for mine. "Come on, baby. Let's finish this."

I allow him to help me up and this time I run onto the field with a lot more confidence, high fiving the captain and the rest of the gang as they congratulate me. My eyes meet my sister's, her proud smile lighting up my entire heart.

A strange sense of belonging washes over me as if the two of us are exactly where we're meant to be.

Unfortunately, after a few more plays, the time to take Chrissy back to the hospital has arrived. It's bittersweet, I'm not ready for it to be over but I'm thankful for the time we were blessed to have.

Once we arrive at the center, I walk over to let the nurses know we are back while Austin gets my sister in bed.

"How did it go?" Dina asks.

"It was wonderful," I tell her, unable to hold back my smile. "She's tired but I think it's exactly what she needed."

The other woman shares my joy. "Good, I'm glad to hear. Are you staying the night?"

I nod.

"Then I'll see you on my rounds soon."

After thanking her for allowing us this day, I head back to my sister's room but stop just outside the door when I see Austin tucking her in. He grabs Gus off her nightstand, pressing the dog's nose against her cheek with a kissing noise that makes her giggle before taking the seat next to her. "Comfortable?"

She nods shakily. "Th-an-k y-ou."

"You're welcome. Did you have fun today?"

"Ve-ry mu-ch."

"Me too. We'll make sure to do it again really soon."

Chrissy says nothing back. She peers into his face, hand struggling to reach for his, much the same way she did with me the other night.

He moves it closer, grasping it in his. "What's on your mind, pretty girl?"

"Ne-ed a... fa-vo-r."

"Anything," he says.

"T-a-ke ca-re of Do-oey?"

Pain infiltrates my chest as I realize today didn't ease her worry as much as I hoped.

"I'm going to take care of both of you."

His promise glides through the air, penetrating my heart while bringing another smile to my sister's face.

I use the opportunity to announce my arrival, clearing my throat as I walk in. "All set. Nurse Dina will check in soon." My voice is gruff and I have no doubt that Austin knows I just heard every word.

With a nod, he pushes to his feet. "I should get going. I have some stuff to take care of before work tomorrow."

"I'll walk you out."

He turns back to my sister. "Later, pretty girl."

"B-ye. Au-sdin."

I follow him out into the hallway and when he turns around, I don't hesitate stepping into him, hugging him close. "Thank you."

"For what?"

"For being you," I answer, my throat thick with emotion. "Today was amazing and it's all thanks to you."

His arms come around me; the strong rhythm of his heartbeat thrumming against my cheek. "It was a good day for us all, Zoey. I'm glad we did it."

"Me too." I lift my face from his chest and gaze up into his dark irises. "For the first time ever, I felt like I was part of a family, like I finally belonged somewhere," the confession falls on nothing more than a whisper.

His hand lifts, cupping my cheek in my favorite gesture. "You belong wherever I am."

His beautiful words dance along my skin and kiss my soul. "Would it be completely unromantic if I told you right now that I am irrevocably falling in love with you?"

A lazy smirk dominates his face. "Would it be unromantic if I told you right now that I already am?"

My smile matches his. "No. It would be perfect."

"Good, because you're perfect." He leans down, brushing his lips to mine, his thumb stroking where his mouth just touched.

"I'm sorry I'm not spending the night again," I apologize, regret heavy in my voice.

"Don't worry about it. We have all the time in the world, Zoey. I'm not going anywhere."

My forehead falls back onto his chest, a groan escaping me. "Stop it. You're too nice."

His chuckle vibrates my cheek before he drops a kiss on my head. "Call me tomorrow?"

I lift my head and nod. "Yeah, tomorrow."

He leaves me with one more heart-stealing kiss, one that I will feel for the rest of the night. "Bye, Zoey girl."

"Bye." I all but practically sigh, sounding like a silly schoolgirl.

He finds it quite amusing if his grin is anything to go by. Once he leaves, I walk back into my sister's room and find her eyes heavy with sleep.

"Tired?"

"Mmm." Is all she can manage.

I sit next to her, taking her hand in mine. "It was a big day but a fun one, wasn't it?"

"The be-st." Her eyes flutter closed, breathing evening out as she's unable to fight the exhaustion any longer.

Leaning over, I press a kiss to her forehead. "Sleep, Chrissy Bee. I'll be here when you wake up."

"Lo-ove you, Do-oey."

"I love you, too. Always."

It isn't long until I fall asleep too, feeling a lot more hope for not only my future but for my sister's, too.

CHAPTER FOURTEEN

Austin

I t's late by the time we roll in from our last call of the night; all of us climbing out of the fire truck at the same time while Cap pulls up in his squad truck next to us.

"Well that was…interesting," Rubin makes the comment, looking more amused than annoyed like the rest of us.

I've been to a lot of fucked-up calls before but being called in to save a pervert from an air vent at a tanning salon because he'd been up there peeking at naked women all day has to take the cake.

"I still say we should have left him there to rot," Cam says, getting agreements from Jake and me.

Cap points at him in warning. "You better hope like hell that fist of yours doesn't come back to bite you in the ass."

The bastard struggled and fought with everything he had once we got up there that he even managed to clip Jake in the face with his boot. That's when Cam let his temper get the best of him and sent a fist to his face.

"What?" Cam feigns ignorance. "I told you it was an accident."

Cap grunts, knowing he's full of shit.

"Besides, he hit Jake first. Look at his mouth all busted up. We should take him to the hospital."

Jake sports more of a minor mark than a busted mouth, but I decide to keep that to myself since Cam is in enough shit.

"He did kick me," Jake adds, barely containing his smirk.

Cap doesn't find it as amusing as the rest of us. "I mean it, Phillips.

I understand that prick had it coming but don't let it happen again. The last thing I need is the commissioner on my ass." He stomps off to his office, entering through the side door.

Once he's out of earshot, we look at each other and burst into laughter. It's how we usually react to one of his fits, which can happen more often than not.

"Whatever, the fucker deserved it," Cam says, refusing to let it go. "I hope he spends a while behind bars and is made someone's bitch. He deserves to know what it feels like to be defenseless like all his victims today."

The thought of all the women who changed unknowingly in front of unwanted eyes sends anger surging through my veins. I'm personally glad Cam got a shot in on him.

Jake nudges my shoulder, his chin lifting in the direction behind me. "Look."

Turning around, I find Chief Ramsey walking across the street toward us. A scowl morphs on my face as I wonder what he's doing here so late. Last I heard, he had taken a leave of absence and it didn't sound like he would be coming back. Not that I can blame him after all he's been through.

"I'm going to head in and start packing up," Rubin mumbles, suddenly becoming uncomfortable. "I'll see you guys later." He barely gives us a chance to bid him a goodbye before bolting into the station.

The three of us get our feet moving, meeting Ramsey just outside the overhead doors.

"Chief." I extend my hand to him first, noticing his unkempt state. His usual clean-cut hair is a greasy mess, his jaw unshaven, and clothes rumpled. He also smells like it's been days since he showered. The one attribute that stands out the most though is the pain that haunts his face, a misery that looks even worse than the last time I saw him at the funeral.

However, he shakes each of our hands, greeting us as he would any other time.

"You here to see Cap?" Cam asks.

"Actually, I came to talk to you boys."

Surprise flares inside of me, my interest piquing. "What can we do for you?"

"I need your help." He exhales a heavy breath, the weight of his pain carrying with it as he runs his hand through his dirty hair. "It's about that night, the one that took my boy."

Guilt rushes to the surface as I relive the few haunting seconds that took Declan's life.

"I need to know everything about that fire," he chokes out. "No one is telling me a goddamn thing other than it was set intentionally. I need answers."

I shake my head. "Look, Chief, with all due respect, I think you should talk to Roper. He's the one running the investigation with the police and can give you more insight."

"Roper is a corrupt son of a bitch who doesn't know his head from his ass," he bites out. "He can't be trusted."

Every muscle in my body tightens, the three of us exchanging a look.

"What do you mean by that?" Jake asks.

"I mean exactly what I said. Why do you think your old man and him never got along? Besides the fact the asshole was always jealous, he couldn't be trusted and your father knew it."

Silence thickens the air as we all absorb this piece of information. I knew Roper was an asshole but corrupt?

"Look, they don't want to tell me anything because I'm too close to the case. Declan..." He trails off, swallowing back his emotion. "He's all I had left. I can't just sit back and do nothing. I need justice. Is there anything, anything at all you can tell me?"

I look over at Jake, seeing the same indecision battling on his face. The information I have came from him, and I decide to let him be the one to share it or not.

"Sorry, Chief. We don't know much more than you," he says in the end. "But Hamilton is in on this too, he's working harder than Roper, and I promise you, if he tells me anything concrete I'll let you know."

The chief nods, satisfied with that answer. "Good." He claps him on the shoulder. "You're a good boy, Ryan. Just like your father."

It's meant as a compliment but by Jake's pained expression all it does is trudge up the hurt he may never overcome from losing his parents. A pain Cam and I share in since they were like family to us as well.

Just then the side door opens, revealing Cap. Tension immediately penetrates the moment, sending the chief backing away.

"You boys keep in touch."

"Will do." I give him a final nod before he turns around and walks off.

Cap joins us, his narrowed eyes following the chief as he climbs back into his car. "What was Ramsey doing here?"

"He wanted to talk to us," Jake answers.

He cocks a brow. "About?"

"He asked if we had any information about the investigation," I respond, refusing to keep anything from him. If there is anyone we can trust in all this, it's Cap.

His lips press together in a thin line. "He shouldn't be bringing you boys into it."

Cam shrugs. "I think he's just desperate for answers like the rest of us."

"I get that but it isn't our department. He needs to let arson do their job."

"He said Roper is corrupt," Jake says, wasting no time. "Is that true?"

Cap levels us with a thoughtful look before finally answering the question. "He's been accused of hiding evidence before."

"Then why the hell is he on this case?" Jake fires back.

"Because nothing was ever proven."

"What do you think?" I speak, curious to know his take on it. "Is he guilty of the accusation?"

"Honestly, I'm not sure. The case he was accused in involved a longtime friend of his, so it's possible, I guess."

"My father thought he was corrupt?" Jake asks, looking for confirmation on what the chief just said.

Cap nods. "He had his suspicions and it's the only reason why I entertain the idea. Dale always had good intuition."

Jake shakes his head. "This is fucked up."

"Listen. Tensions are running high right now with this bastard on the loose but it's not for you boys to worry about. Roper isn't the only one working this case. Police have a hand in it too and so does Hamilton. We have to trust that justice will prevail. In the meantime, we keep doing our job while they do theirs. Understand?"

We all nod in agreement but I don't miss the knowledge in Jake's eyes. He's not letting this go. Not by a long shot.

"Are you ever going to tell us what happened between the two of you?" Cam asks the one question that we all have at some point.

"Nope."

We grunt, knowing it was a long shot.

"Now go on and get out of here," he says, clapping me on the shoulder. "Go get some sleep."

At the dismissal, we head to our lockers to grab our bags then leave for home. The entire drive to my house my mind spins with everything the chief revealed, my gut twisting into a giant knot as I think about how wrecked he looked. How lost in grief he still is.

It conjures up images from the night we lost Declan. The look on his face, the fear that washed over him seconds before the flames swallowed him right before my eyes.

The guilt at times is still overwhelming and it doesn't help that the person responsible for it all is still out there. It has us all on edge as we wait for his next move, having no idea what destruction he will leave in his wake.

My morbid thoughts take a quick turn when I arrive home to find a familiar car parked in my driveway. Climbing out of my truck, shock renders me for all of a second when I see Zoey on my porch swing, swaying back and forth.

"Surprise," she says, wearing my favorite smile. The dim light casts a glow that makes her look like the angel I know she is.

My angel.

I hang back by my truck, arm slung over the open door. "What did I do to deserve this?"

Standing to her feet, she walks to the end of the porch, looking quite proud of herself. "I left the bar early to see my sister and found out she had a great day so I decided to come spend the night with my favorite guy. I kinda forgot you were on the late shift," she adds sheepishly.

"How long have you been waiting out here for?"

That slender shoulder lifts in a shrug. "An hour or two."

"That long?" Remorse fills my chest, hating to know she's been sitting here in the dark by herself.

She rests against the column, her pretty eyes holding mine in the dark. "Don't you know I'd wait an eternity for you, Hawke?"

The soft confession puts me in motion. Slamming my truck door, I collect several long strides, closing the distance between us before taking her in my arms and holding her close. The feel of her against me eases the turmoil I was feeling minutes ago. "I'm so fucking glad you're here."

She senses the change in my voice, her head pulling back. "Hey"— her hand reaches up, fingers fanning my jaw—"everything okay?"

"It is now." I don't give her the chance to question me further. My mouth claims hers, dominating it in a desperate attempt to chase away the haunting images that I can't seem to erase.

Her arms curl around my neck as she melts against me, breathy moans leaving her in a rush.

My hands slip to her tight ass, lifting her off her feet. She wraps her legs around my waist as I carry her inside, heading straight for the shower.

Her mouth is relentless as I lean over to turn on the water, lips trailing along my jaw before nipping my ear sharply.

Growling, I thrust us both under the spray, the water and my own primal need immersing us further into this pool of desire we constantly find ourselves in. I pull at her drenched tank top, ripping the straps from her shoulders before tugging it down and taking a pink nipple into my mouth.

A harsh whimper breaches her lips, back arching to offer me more.

"So fucking pretty," I groan, moving to the other nipple, tongue lashing as I drink the hot water rushing down the firm mounds.

"Austin," my name falls past her lips like a seductive melody. "Now. Please, I need you."

The need drowning her desperate plea only fuels my own. I make quick work of the rest of our clothes then pin her against the wall, arranging her legs to hang in the crook of my arms before driving up inside of her.

Her cry of pleasure pierces the air, feeding the hunger raging within my blood.

"Goddamn, Zoey. I've missed you." I drop my forehead onto her shoulder, losing myself in the feel of her. Between all the late shifts and her time at the hospital, it feels like an eternity since I've had her like this.

"Me too, so much."

Steam blankets the air, thick and heavy, our bodies merging in a single effort to drive out every single thing around us. Nothing matters in this moment but this…us.

It doesn't take long before we're both propelled into mindless oblivion and it drowns out every haunting thought that plagued me earlier.

Afterward, I take to washing her body, cherishing every part of her before turning off the water and carrying her to my room.

Comfortable silence settles over us as we lie amongst the rumpled sheets of my bed, her body draped over mine while my fingers skim her slender spine.

Rolling onto her stomach, she props a fist on my chest, resting her chin on it as she pins me with those startling blue irises. "What was wrong earlier?"

I consider lying to her again, the last thing I want to do is bother her with shit that neither of us can change but know it would be pointless. She knows me too well.

"Just work stuff. Nothing you need to worry about."

The answer doesn't suffice, her disappointment reflecting back at me. "You're always there for me, Austin, let me be here for you."

A resigned breath escapes my chest, carrying the burden I feel with it. "I saw the chief tonight and it just brought back everything I've been trying to forget."

"Declan?" she asks gently.

I nod, guilt searing my veins all over again. "Weeks have passed yet it feels like just yesterday he was just with us, fighting for the very thing he died for."

She reaches out, touching my jaw in a comforting gesture. "I can imagine it's hard to get used to."

"Yeah. It's not the same without him." I swallow hard and tell her what haunts me most. "I've run that night through my head so many goddamn times, Zoey. Wondering what I could have done differently. He was just a rookie for christ's sake...too eager maybe but he didn't deserve to die."

"Of course he didn't, but you have to know that's not on you, Austin. His death is not your fault."

It's something I've tried telling myself time and time again but being his lieutenant it was my job to watch out for him and no matter which way I spin it, I failed. It's something I'm not sure I will ever be able to forgive myself for.

"Are the police any closer to catching the arsonist?"

"No." Frustration burns inside of me as I think about just how far they are from catching the bastard. "These fires are unlike anything I've ever encountered, there's no telling what this asshole will do next."

Silence settles over us with the heavy moment, my gaze on the ceiling as I fight off the images trying to pull me under again.

"Promise me something," she whispers, fear suddenly edging her voice.

My eyes revert back to hers. "Anything."

"Promise me that you'll always be careful, that you'll always come back to me," the words are choked out, emotion bleeding within them.

"Always." My hand cups her cheek, the concern in her eyes tearing apart my chest. "It'd take a lot more than a fire to keep me away, Zoey girl. I'd walk through the raging depths of hell to come back to you."

A smile tugs at her pretty pink lips, easing the worry that gripped her face moments ago. "You always say the most perfect things."

Stretching up, she presses her lips to mine. My fingers curl around her neck as I deepen the kiss, claiming what I will never allow another to have.

What will always ever be mine.

Only when I sense her need for her air do I pull back, my thumb brushing her swollen lips. "Sleep, Zoey girl, and know I'll always be right here waiting for you."

She rests her head back on my chest, wrapping her body around mine. "I love you," the words drift through the dark room on the softest whisper but the impact they hold is deafening.

"I love you, too."

It isn't long until I hear her breathing even out, the rhythmic sound driving out any lingering turmoil, bringing me the peace I had been searching for.

CHAPTER FIFTEEN

Zoey

A long, exhausted breath escapes me as I click the lock in place on the bar door and flip the sign to closed. "What a night," I sigh, walking toward Frank while he shuts off the remaining lights.

"Damn right it was but look at it this way, we made bank."

I smile, pleased with the number I saw after cash out. "Trust me, I'm not complaining. I'll take sore feet any day for the money we pulled in tonight."

It couldn't have come at a better time because the hospital bill this month was much higher than usual with all the new medication we have been trying for Chrissy. It's been financially draining but thankfully the newest one seems to be working so far. Let's hope it stays that way. I'm ready to get her out of there and start building our life together.

Frank slings an arm around my shoulders as we head out the back door, walking me to my car like he does whenever Austin isn't here. "You headed to go see that man of yours now?"

I can't deny the way my heart leaps to hear him call Austin mine. "Not tonight. He's been pulling some overtime lately so I'm going to let him get some sleep and stay with Chrissy again."

Though, I'm tempted to stop by his place in the morning and surprise him with another session like I did yesterday. Thanks to the key he gave me last week, I caught him while he was in the shower and it was the most unforgettable experience of my life. My body comes alive just thinking about it.

"You tell that sweet girl I said hi."

"Will do." After a kiss to his cheek, I hop in my car and drive away. My gaze drifts to the clock to see it's half past two and it only has my eyes growing heavier.

Lowering my window, I crank my music as loud as it can go, blaring it all the way to the hospital to keep me awake. It does the job.

Just as I pull into a spot at the hospital, it begins raining, big fat drops falling heavy and hard. I rush inside the building, shaking myself dry before walking into the elevator and heading up to the third floor like I do every time I visit.

Some days this is so routine I feel like I'm stuck in that movie *Groundhog Day*. Where Bill Murray's character wakes up every morning only to keep living the same day he did before. As tiring as it can be, I know it won't always be like this. One day Chrissy and I will be living together again, hopefully sooner rather than later.

As the thought filters through my mind, an image of Austin's house pops into my head, the three of us having the life I've always dreamed about. The hope that inflates my heart is undeniable.

When the elevator pings with my arrival, I step out with a wistful smile only to come to a hard stop at the nurses' station when I see them all gathered together, tears of sorrow streaming down their faces. I immediately know something has happened to one of the patients.

"Dina?" I call her name gently, finding her amongst the crowd as I walk closer.

Everyone's eyes swing to me and the moment Dina's gaze meets mine, it stops me in my tracks again. The way she looks at me with such devastation has my heart plummeting straight to my stomach.

It's not just a patient.

A terrified breath traps in the confines of my chest, thundering in my ears as I feel the walls around me closing in.

She starts toward me, slowly and regretfully.

"No." I retreat from her approach, dread weighing every step as I try to turn back time, to walk back out of here and change the last several seconds.

"Zoey," she cries, continuing forward. "Please stop."

I shake my head, bracing my hands out in front of me to keep her from getting any closer. "Stay back." The words are choked out, my breathing coming out short and fast. "Please, stop."

"We tried to call you a few minutes ago," she says, emotion thick in her voice. "She went into cardiac arrest, we did all we could do, but we couldn't re—"

"Shut up!" I yell, a sob falling with it. "Just shut up!" Unable to bear hearing another word, I take the stairs, refusing to wait for the elevator.

My legs are quick, strides lost in motion as I flee from the hospital and out into the rainy night. I pass my car in a blur of movement, my tennis shoes eating up the concrete as darkness threatens to close in.

It's like a nightmare speeding through me, colliding on a dark, deserted highway. I run so hard and so fast that there's no sense of time—no sense of reality, because what awaits me is unthinkable—unfathomable.

It can't be true.

"Lo-ve y-ou, Do-o-ey."

The last words she spoke to me emerge, sending me to my knees in the desolate streets. My head drops back on my shoulders, a sob of agony exploding past my lips. The sound of my pain pierces the night as I will the rain to wash away the brutal reality, but all it does is drown my soul in a black pool of despair, leaving me to die along with my sister.

CHAPTER SIXTEEN

Austin

The incessant chime of my cellphone yanks me from a deep sleep. Groaning, I roll over and feel across my nightstand, fumbling for the annoying device.

If it's Cam bragging about the pussy he got tonight I'm going to kill him.

Once my fingers curl around it, I bring it to my ear, not bothering to look at the caller ID. "What?" I bark but it's weak with exhaustion.

"Austin?"

The crying female voice has me bolting upright. "Who is this?" I pull the phone away, looking at the number but don't recognize it.

"It's Sam."

"Sam?" I repeat, trying to clear the fog from my mind. My eyes dart to the clock, seeing it's the middle of the night and know this can't be good. "What's wrong?" Worry plagues me as I think about Jase, praying I'm not about to hear that something has happened to him. I can't take losing another one.

"Is Zoey with you?" she asks.

A scowl forms on my face. "No. She's with Chrissy. Why?"

Another sob fills the line, adding to the fear in my chest.

"Sam, what the hell is going on? You're scaring the shit out of me."

Jase comes on the line just then. "Austin, man. You need to find Zoey."

"I just told Sam, she's at the hospital with her sister."

"No, she's not." His tone has lead settling in my gut. "Sam just got a call from the hospital. She's one of the emergency contacts on Chrissy's medical form. She"—he pauses, his hard swallow audible— "she's gone, man. She passed away earlier tonight."

Grief slams into me, fisting the organ in my chest. "No." I shake my head, refusing to believe it. "That's not possible. I just saw her this morning. You must have heard wrong."

"I'm sorry. Sam just got the call from the head nurse. Apparently, Zoey ran out of there. She wouldn't even hear what happened and no one can get a hold of her."

Desperation has me bolting from the bed and throwing my jeans on in a hurry.

"You still there?" he asks.

"Yeah, I'm here." I can barely manage the words through my re-stricted throat. "I'm on my way out. I'll call or text when I find her."

"Sam and I will be on the next flight out. We'll see you soon."

I hang up, unable to say one more word through the despair suffo-cating me. It's storming as I run out to my truck, lightning charging the gloomy sky. I peel out of my long driveway, tires spinning on the wet gravel as my wipers fight through the heavy rainfall. I relentlessly call Zoey's cellphone only to get no answer like everyone else.

"Fuck!" I slam my fist into the dash, fighting the burn in my chest and eyes as I try to grasp the devastating reality I've just been told.

A beautiful, young girl gone. A girl I didn't know long but affected me as strongly as her sister did. I grind my teeth against the pain and know it pales in comparison to what Zoey must be going through right now. The thought only amps up my concern to find her.

The first place I check is her apartment but find her car isn't there. Regardless, I jump from the truck, leaving it running, and ring her buzzer a few times just to be sure. When I'm greeted with silence, I drive to the bar next only to find all the lights off.

Fear collides with misery as I wonder where the hell she could be. Having no other choice, I head to the hospital to see if I can retrace her steps. Relief fills my chest when I find her car parked on the street.

I barely shut off my truck before I'm running into the hospital and heading up to the third floor. My rain-soaked hair drips into my face, chest heaving heavy and hard as I try to calm my raging heartbeat.

Dina is there as I step off the elevator, her eyes red and swollen. "Thank God," she cries, hurrying over to me. "I would have called you sooner but I didn't have your number."

"Where is she?" I ask, scanning the halls for her.

"Who?"

"Zoey?"

She falters, concern pinching her expression. "She's not with you?"

"No. Her car is outside."

"Well she's not here. She never came back."

Dread settles over me once again, sending me back to the elevator. "Goddamn it."

"Austin, wait." Dina catches up to me just as I hit the button. "When you find her please tell her..." She trails off, voice cracking. "Tell her I'm sorry. We tried. We really did."

"What the hell happened, Dina?" My throat burns like a mother-fucker as I ask the one question I can't fathom. "How can she be gone? I just saw her this morning and she was fine. She looked...perfect."

Guilt darkens her eyes. "She had a bad reaction to the medication. She went into cardiac arrest and we couldn't revive her." A sob falls from her before she claps a hand over her mouth to stifle it. "She was just too tired, Austin. She couldn't fight anymore."

The grief fisting my chest passes back and forth like a ball of fire but I shove it aside, focusing only on Zoey right now. It's all I can take at the moment, the other reality hurts too fucking much.

"What was Zoey wearing?" I ask.

"A thin pink sweater and white jeans."

"Thanks." Once the elevator pings, I climb back on.

"Please let me know when you find her."

I give her a nod just as the door closes. Heavy rain assaults me once again when I walk back outside. I look back and forth, trying to figure out which direction to take next. To my left, I spot a homeless man taking shelter under the bus stop awning.

I head his way in a rush, kneeling before his huddled form.

He flinches, cowering away from me.

"I'm not going to hurt you," I yell to be heard over the rain. "I just need to know if you saw a blonde woman run out of here tonight. She was wearing a pink sweater and white jeans."

A flash of knowledge enters the other man's eyes but he hesitates, his narrowed gaze assessing. "What do you want with her?"

"She's my girlfriend and needs help. Please, if you know where she is..."

He must see something he trusts because after a few agonizing seconds he finally gives me the information I'm desperate for. "She ran that way," he says, pointing left. "If I were you, I'd take your truck. I've never seen someone run so fast and it didn't look like she was stopping anytime soon."

That doesn't have me feeling any better. I push to stand and hand him a few bills, hoping he uses it to get him a dry place to sleep for the night.

Relief and gratitude fill his tired eyes. "Thanks, mister."

I head for my truck and put in a call to a friend at the police department.

"Cunningham," he answers, voice thick with sleep.

"Denver, it's Austin. I need your help."

"What's wrong?" he asks, sounding more alert.

I explain what's happened and give him Zoey's description. "Whoever is on call tonight, can you have them keep an eye out for her?"

"Yeah, I'll put in the call now. Keep in touch if you find her first."

"I will. Thanks." After hanging up, I pull away from the curb and start in the direction I was given. The continuous rain leaves me no choice but to lower my windows, my gaze scanning the streets and back alleys.

Block after block, my hope dwindles. It isn't until about a mile from the hospital that something catches my attention, a flash of white enveloped in darkness. Despite the woman's crouched position, I have no doubt it's her.

My foot is heavy on the brake, truck skidding to a halt as I jump out into the downpour. "Zoey!" Her name pushes from my throat, penetrating the hammering rain as I race down the dark alleyway.

Knees hugged to her chest and face turned away from me, she doesn't acknowledge my call.

I drop down before her, lifting her face to mine. "Look at me." A sharp breath impales my lungs at her vacant, red-rimmed eyes. Soaked to the bone, devastation clings to her like second skin.

She looks so lost, so…broken.

She stares back at me like she doesn't even know who I am, her drenched body trembling violently.

"Zoey girl, talk to me." My hand strokes her wet cheek, willing her to see me—to feel me.

Just then something flashes in her eyes, the first sign of life, but it's a painful one. "Help me." The two words quiver past her lips, the most agonized breath falling with it. "Please, help me."

The plea finishes me. I pull her into my arms, holding her shuddering body. "I've got you, baby. I'm here now."

A sob shatters her chest, her devastation echoing through the deserted alley and decimating what's left of my heart. For the first time since hearing the news, I allow my own tears to fall, sharing in her grief that will no doubt haunt me for the rest of my life.

CHAPTER SEVENTEEN

Zoey

There's a gaping hole in my chest as I slowly come awake, my soul submerged in a sea of heartbreak. I dread opening my eyes, fearing the reality that awaits me. A reality I'm not sure I will ever be able to face.

The unavoidable happens anyway, my swollen eyes fluttering open. I squint at the sun dripping in through the floor to ceiling windows and take in my surroundings, realizing I'm in Austin's bedroom.

Images from last night emerge, catapulting me into a nightmare I will never wake up from, a life I don't want to accept. Not without my baby sister.

My watery gaze wanders over the room, trying to find something to cling to before I'm dragged even deeper into this hell.

It's then I find Austin. He stands strong and tall, leaning against a window and wearing nothing but a pair of jeans. His arms are crossed over his bare chest as he watches me, the misery in his eyes reflecting the one in my heart.

For a single moment, I'm anchored and my world stops spinning into a dark madness. "What time is it?" I croak, my throat feeling damaged from the aftermath of last night.

"Noon." His voice is as solemn as his expression. He moves to the nightstand and passes me a glass of water along with some aspirin. "Here. Take these."

I carefully sit up and comply, the cool liquid burning my raw throat. Afterward, I put the glass down and look away, unable to bear seeing the disappointment I know he must be feeling at the way he found me.

Events of last night are muddled at best, my mind not wanting to revisit, to remember the tragedy I was faced with. Regardless of my best effort, the pain is too raw and real to ignore.

"Tell me it's not true," I whisper, sucking in a painful breath. "Tell me my baby sister isn't dead." Speaking the devastating words has a sob tumbling past my lips.

Austin drops down next to me, pulling me into his strong arms, but I don't feel their usual comfort, I'm too cold. Too...dead inside.

"I'm sorry, Zoey girl. I wish I could tell you what we both want to hear but I can't." He sounds as defeated as I feel. He may not have known my sister long but he loved her too, as much as she loved him. "We will get through this though. I promise you that."

Right now that seems impossible. Days ago I had so much hope for the future. We were supposed to have more time to build the life together I always promised her, and now I will never get that chance. I will never get the chance to make it right.

A knock on the front door breaks us from our embrace. "I'll be right back." He drops a kiss on my head before climbing to his feet and leaving the room.

I pull the covers closer around me, reaching for a measure of warmth but there is none to grasp. Everything feels a million miles away, a never-ending tunnel of heartbreak I'll be lost in forever.

"Zoey."

My head snaps up at the familiar voice, surprise rendering me speechless for all of a second when I find my best friend standing in the doorway. "Sam?"

We move at the same time, both of us falling into each other's arms.

"I'm so sorry, Zoey. So sorry." Her sorrow runs as deep as my own. She's known Chrissy since she was a baby. If anyone can understand the depth of my pain, it's her.

"How did you find out?" I ask, lifting my head from her shoulder.

"Dina called me after you left the hospital."

My eyes close as I'm reminded of those few fateful seconds before I ran off. I didn't even give her a chance to explain. I couldn't bear to hear it. I didn't want to believe it. I still don't.

Austin and Jase appear in the doorway just then, Jase walking in to drop a kiss on my cheek. "I'm sorry about your sister, Zoey."

"Thanks," I whisper. "Thank you both for coming."

Sam reaches for my hand, covering it with hers. "I wouldn't be anywhere else."

She's always been there for me through the most trying times and right now I need her more than ever before.

"I don't know what to do," I say, feeling lost and broken. "I don't know where to go from here."

Austin clears his throat. "I spoke with Dina this morning. Chrissy..." He pauses, taking a hard swallow. "She's still there if you want to see her and say goodbye."

My heart sinks at the thought. The last words my sister and I spoke to one another were "I love you," I kissed her goodbye then walked out with the intention of seeing her hours later. A part of me wants to remember her that way. I'm not sure I can handle seeing her cold, lifeless body because then I'll have no choice but to accept this.

"What do you think?" Sam asks gently.

Despite my internal battle, I find myself nodding. As hard as this will be, I need to do it. I need to see her. To tell her I love her one last time.

We all end up going, something I'm thankful for, because right now I need all the support I can get. To keep me from being swallowed into this black hole I've found myself in.

Austin keeps me close, tucked into his side as we enter the hospital. His comfort and presence is my life preserver in the devastation I drown in.

When the elevator pings with our destination, dread settles over me. It's everything I can do to put one foot in front of the other as I step out.

Dina spots us from the nurses' station, her grief as raw and fresh as it was last night. She pulls me into her arms, hugging me close. "I'm sorry, honey. We did everything we could."

"I know." My words are as mechanical as my arms, my mind and heart lost in darkness.

She grasps my face between her hands. "She fought a long time, Zoey. She's not in pain anymore."

They are words meant to comfort but they don't bring any peace. In all fairness, nothing can, not at this time and maybe not ever.

"She's back in her room for you to have some privacy. If you're ready?"

I want to rage that I'm not ready. That I will never be ready for this, but instead I find myself nodding, knowing it's inevitable.

Austin pulls me in close again, pushing me to get my feet moving while Sam walks on my other side, holding my hand. Every step is weighted as I cling to their silent strength, praying it can get me through this.

"We'll wait out here," he says, stopping just outside her closed door. "Unless you want us in there with you?"

"I'll be fine."

It's a lie, a big fat lie. I'm not fine and I won't ever be.

His large warm hands frame my face before he leans down, brushing his lips across my cold ones, just a feather of a touch but it instills a small measure of peace into my shattered heart.

"I've got you, Zoey girl. Always and forever. Never forget that. If you need me, I'm right here."

It was the exact words I needed to hear in this moment.

Sam pulls me in for a hug next. "Take as much time as you need."

After a deep breath, I grasp the handle then walk in, letting the door close behind me. For the first few moments I don't look over in her direction. I keep my gaze straight ahead, my feet moving numbly as I stare out a window that she did so many times before.

In this moment, I wonder what she thought about as she did. Did she wish to be out there with the rest of the world? Was she lonely and sad, despite my best efforts?

The thought only adds to the sorrow gripping my heart. Once I make it to the side of her bed, I finally find the courage to look at her and the sight of her is heart stopping.

Her body isn't tensed or curled in an unusual painful form as it used to be. It's relaxed, her face soft and peaceful. If I didn't know better, I'd swear she was sleeping.

"Hey, Chrissy bee." The words grate past my throat as I reach for her hand to find it ice cold. It drives the painful reminder home that she is not sleeping. That she will never open her eyes again.

Gus sits next to her pillow and it's the stuffed animal, the dream I didn't have a chance to make a reality that sends me crumbling to my knees on a sob. Devastation consumes me as I drop my face on her lifeless hand, wishing she could feel my tears and love.

"I'm so sorry. So sorry I wasn't here with you."

It's something I never wanted to happen. That if or when this time ever came I would be there, holding her hand and making sure she knew she was loved beyond measure. Now I will never get that chance.

"I'll love you forever, Chrissy bee."

My sorrow consumes the room as I say goodbye to the one person I lived and breathed for. The only family I ever truly had.

A girl I will never be whole without again.

Hours later, I'm back in Austin's bed, wrapped in blankets with Gus on my lap and Sam next to me. She holds my hand as I stare vacantly at the wall, lost somewhere between numbness and grief.

Eventually, Austin, Sam, and Jase came into the room too, and watching their goodbyes hurt my heart even more. Since then, I've been shoved deeper into this grief-stricken state, unable to grasp that this has become my reality.

Before we left the hospital, the doctor prescribed me something that would help me "cope better." It hasn't. A part of me wonders if I will ever feel warm again. If my heart will ever beat the same way without my sister.

"Can I get you some more tea?" Sam asks gently, continuing to be attentive while Austin and Jase are out getting something for dinner.

The thought of eating anything right now has my hollow stomach churning.

I shake my head, feeling too broken to speak.

"Is there anything I can do to make this better?"

The crack in her voice has me finally looking over at her, my battered heart bleeding at the helplessness on her face. The same defeat I've seen on Austin's all day. I'm hurting so badly and dragging them down with me.

I squeeze her hand, her warm temperature a contradiction to my ice cold one. "Just being here with me helps."

She flashes me a sympathetic smile but it does nothing to hide the remorse etched on her face.

"Tell me something good," I whisper. "Tell me about the wedding."

"We sent out the invitations yesterday," she says, a small note of excitement entering her voice. "All I have left is finalizing the delivery of the peaches with the McNallys."

"It's going to be amazing, Sam. I can't wait to be a part of it," I tell her, meaning it.

"Me too. It's hard to believe that only months ago we were bidding on Jase and Austin at that auction, isn't it?"

"Yeah, funny how that worked out." My response is halfhearted at best as I think about the last few months I've spent with the man who stole not only my heart so quickly but also my sister's.

"I'm glad you have him, Zoey, especially right now. I can see how much you two care about each other."

"I more than care about him," I tell her softly. "I'm in love with him." The confession flows freely past my lips but is weighted with sadness.

"Then what's wrong?"

It takes me a moment to answer as I try to find the right words. "I don't know. I guess I just feel bad. From the moment we met all he's shown me is love and affection and all he's gotten from me is grief and responsibility. Now this…" I shake my head. "I feel like all I ever do is hurt him. I'm hurting him so much right now."

"We're all hurting right now, Zoey, but that's not on you. It's never been on you. Austin knew what he was getting into when it came to Chrissy. He loves you, regardless of your hardships. I can see it."

"For how long?" I ask, voicing my biggest fear. "How long can he keep going like this, because I don't know if or when I will ever get over this, Sam. How do I go on living without my baby sister?"

She pulls me into her arms as another sob breaks from me. "You cling to the people who love you. You let us help you through it and we will. I promise, Zoey. I won't leave your side. Near or far, I'll always be here."

Her friendship means a lot but the truth is no one will be able erase this unfathomable pain. It's embedded into my soul forever.

CHAPTER EIGHTEEN

Austin

I sip the amber liquid from the tumbler I clutch in my hand, relishing the burn in my throat that spreads to my chest as I stand on my porch, staring out across my property.

It's hard to believe that days ago I was making plans on how to make my home wheelchair accessible so I could give Zoey and her sister the life they always wanted, but now that day will never come and I'm not sure how to accept that.

I've witnessed death too many times to count; it comes with being a firefighter. We can't save everyone no matter how hard we try.

I've held car crash victims in my arms as they bled to death, promising that I would tell their loved ones their final words. I've pulled a child's charred body from the ashes of a fiery destruction and even watched one of my own be taken right before my eyes. Each and every loss has brought pain and regret, but nothing has hurt as much as watching the woman I love lost in grief as we buried her little sister this week. Nothing I say or do can ease her pain and I feel so fucking helpless.

Sam and Jase never left our sides until this morning. Having them here helped a lot, especially Sam. She was able to give something to Zoey I couldn't. I try not to let that sting because she's known her longer but I'll admit it sucks. This whole fucking situation sucks.

Right when I thought things couldn't get any worse, Jake called a few hours ago to tell me the arsonist has struck again. This time, a convenience store with people still inside. Most survived, all but one.

Grinding my teeth, I take the last sip of liquor but it does nothing to calm the rage and helplessness I feel.

"Fuck!" My arm whips back, throwing the now empty glass against my house, shattering it.

The destruction brings Zoey out of the house, her eyes dropping to the shards of glass before they come up to mine. My outburst puts even more sadness on her beautiful face, adding to the guilt residing in my chest.

"Sorry," I choke out.

Without a word, she walks up to me, wrapping her arms around my waist. The feel of her slender frame against my rigid one brings a slight reprieve to the hell we've found ourselves in. I pull her in close, breathing a little easier as the scent of her shampoo penetrates my senses.

"I'm the one who's sorry," she whispers. "I'm hurting so much and dragging you down with me."

"That's not true," I tell her, hating the remorse in her voice.

She lifts her face from my chest and the misery in her eyes is almost enough to bring me to my fucking knees. "Yes, it is, and it needs to stop."

There's a shift in her tone, a change in her expression that has fear simmering across every inch of my skin. "What are you saying?"

"I think it's best I go back to my place for a little while."

"No," the word rolls sharply off my tongue.

"Look, I appreciate everything you've done for me, Austin, but I can't keep doing this to you. You haven't even been back to work since…" She trails off, unable to finish that sentence.

"I don't give a shit about any of that. I only care about you, about this right here." I hug her closer, driving my point home.

"So do I. Which is why I need to do this. I need to get better for us."

The thought of her walking away has panic gripping my chest. "Don't do this, Zoey. Don't push me away."

Regret darkens her irises, mixing with the lingering pain. "I'm not walking away from you or us. This isn't goodbye. I just need some time, Austin. Time to find my way out of this. Can you give me that? Will you wait for me?"

The plea has me swallowing the argument that dangles in the back of my throat, my mind and heart refusing this decision but my hand lifting to her face regardless. "I'm not going anywhere. I'll give you this space, Zoey, but only for so long. Eventually, I'm coming for you."

She graces me with a weak smile before turning her head and pressing her lips against my palm. "I'll hold you to it, Hawke."

I frame her beautiful sad face, tilting it up to mine to claim her lips, wishing I could beg her to stay, to make her see we are stronger together. Instead, I give her what she asked for. Somehow, I step back and manage to let her go. It's one of the hardest fucking things I've ever done.

The moment she walks away, my world turns dark.

CHAPTER NINETEEN

Zoey

The hardest part of losing someone you love isn't saying goodbye, it's learning how to live without them.

How does one go on living when the person they lived for is gone? Chrissy was my purpose; everything I did, including owning this bar, was for her.

I look around the crowded establishment, trying to find a sense of normalcy, but all of it feels wrong because nothing in my life is normal anymore. Not without my baby sister and not without the man I love.

A week has passed since I left Austin's house and every second I have regretted it. We've texted every day but it hasn't been enough. The truth is, I need him. I need him so much but I couldn't keep hurting him the way I was. I saw the defeat on his face, the helplessness in his eyes. He didn't know how to help me but what he fails to realize is nothing or no one can. I need to do this on my own. The problem is, I don't know how. I'm lost in this dark place and don't know how to find my way out.

My hand moves to the locket around my neck that holds some of my sister's ashes. Something I chose at the funeral home while making arrangements. Most of the events from that time are a blur but not this. Picking this necklace is the most vivid moment, standing out amongst the rest. In some small way, it makes me feel closer to her, to carry her around with me wherever I go. Close to my heart where she will always belong.

The funeral was small. Only my closest friends, which included

Austin's friends, and some of the nurses from the center. Even his parents came, but not my mother.

Anger burns through me, colliding with the grief. She didn't even answer her phone. I had to leave a message. If there was anything left between us to salvage it's unsalvageable now. As far as I'm concerned, she's dead to me.

"Hey, lady. Where the hell is my drink?"

The irritated voice knocks me from my thoughts and I realize I'm standing in the middle of the bar, staring at nothing. I look over at the customer who has been waiting for his drink since I walked away from his table. "Sorry. It's coming."

He grumbles his annoyance behind me as I walk up to the counter, placing down the empty glass I was carrying.

"A Scotch on the rocks," I tell Frank, my gaze avoiding his. I know exactly what I will find there and it's not something I can deal with right now.

I feel his disapproval anyway, his eyes on me the entire time as he grabs a tumbler and shoves some ice in it. "You need to go home, sweetheart. It's too soon."

I shake my head, telling him the same thing I have been since coming in. "I'm fine. It's time."

"Says who?"

My eyes finally lift to his. "Says me. I don't want to be alone anymore, Frank." Emotion bubbles up my throat but I manage to swallow it back.

Understanding flashes across his face as he nods. "All right then, no more arguments from me." He places the glass down on my tray. "Go get 'em, kid."

My smile is weak as I lift the tray and head toward the table, only to have it slip from my hand and shatter at my feet.

"Shit!" I kneel down, tears of frustration pricking my eyes as I pick up the large chunks.

Don't cry, Zoey. Not here. Now now.

No matter how many times I say the mantra, I'm not fooling my-self. Frank is right. I shouldn't be here.

Just as the thought emerges, a warm, gentle hand wraps around my wrist. A touch I would know anywhere.

My heart falters, seizing in my chest as I look up to find Austin before me, his kind and patient gaze anchoring my broken heart. "Time's up, Zoey girl."

The little composure I managed to hold onto all day shatters as I throw my arms around his neck on a sob. He sweeps my feet out from under me, encompassing me with the love and strength I desperately need. I have no shame in it, my face tucking into his neck and body clinging to his.

"I'm taking her out of here," he says to Frank.

"Good. Don't let her come back for a while. I've got things covered."

I want to thank him, to tell him how sorry I am for the mess I've made, but I'm too lost in my grief to mutter one word.

Austin carries me out to his truck, situating me inside. After belting me in, he leans down and presses his lips to mine. It's the softest touch but the power of it rocks me to my core, the first burst of life finding its way into my dead heart.

I fist his shirt with both my hands, pulling him closer in my vain attempt for more. Groaning, he gives me what I want, deepening the kiss.

There's so much I want to tell him. So much I want to explain, but right now, this is all that matters. His mouth on mine, breathing love back into my soul.

His lips begin to slow their relentless assault before he pulls back, resting his forehead on mine, his deep, dark eyes grounding me. "Let's go home."

Home.

That one word just changed the magnitude of a minute. Suddenly, in the midst of my own despair, I'm no longer alone. No longer…lost.

At my nod, he closes the door then climbs in on his side. I watch the bar fade away in the mirror, feeling a sense of relief the further we get.

My head rests against the window, all the sleepless nights weighing heavily on me, and before I know it, we are turning on the gravel road that leads to Austin's house. Even in the strong silence, his presence next to me remains strong, like a compass guiding my way.

When we arrive home, he puts the truck in park but keeps it running, the headlights illuminating his house before us.

I turn to face him, my eyes seeking his in the darkness. "I'm sorry I left." The apology falls on a whisper as I attempt to give him the explanation he deserves. "I'm so used to doing things on my own, especially the hard times, that I thought that's what I needed to do to get through this."

"Did it work?" he asks.

"No, and right now I'm not sure what the answer is or if I'll ever find it." Defeat is as heavy in my voice as it is in my heart. "Nothing in my life makes sense anymore, Austin. I feel like I don't even know who I am."

He reaches across the console, his fingers brushing across my wet cheek. "You and me, Zoey girl. We make sense."

His response washes over me in a tidal wave of truth, the conviction in his tone driving home every word. I lean into his touch, seeking his comfort. "You're right, and I missed you so much this past week. I didn't want to leave but I was scared. I still am."

"Of what?"

"Of hurting you. That I'll never be able to get through this." I gaze back at him, my breath shuddering with emotion. "How am I supposed to let her go?" The question tumbles past my lips on a sob.

Sympathy flashes in his eyes, his thumb wiping away my flowing tears. "You don't have to. Just because she's gone, Zoey, doesn't mean you have to stop loving her. This pain, the loss, it's just going to take time. It's not going to go away overnight."

My eyes close, fearing it will never fade. Everything still feels so raw and fresh, even this many days later.

"I have something for you."

My eyes spring open at the announcement.

Releasing my cheek, he reaches in the backseat and pulls out a wrapped present, placing it on my lap.

"What is it?" I ask, surprised by the gesture.

"Open it."

I pull the thick white ribbon, unraveling it before pulling apart each corner. What I reveal has my breath stalling. A sleek black camera. One of the best on the market. I've always wanted one but could never afford it.

I look over at Austin, completely speechless.

"You once told me your dream was to capture the beauty of the world behind a lens. You said it gave you a sense of purpose."

My heart soars as he repeats every word I told him on our first date.

"You put those dreams on hold to love your sister and give her everything you could. You did that, Zoey, and now it's your turn. Find that feeling again, find your purpose."

I stare down at the camera of my dreams, seeing the endless possibilities I could capture.

"And while you do, bring me with you." His voice retracts my gaze back to his as he speaks again. "Because I need you as much as you need me. I want everything that comes with loving you, even the hardest and saddest times."

The beautiful words send me over the console and into his arms. "Thank you," I whisper, hugging him tight. "Thank you so much. Not only for this camera but for also being here for me, because you're right, I do need you so much. And you can have me for as long as you want me."

His arms come around me, sure and strong. "Forever, Zoey girl. That's how long I want you for."

The vow works its way into my heart, cementing the broken pieces.

His lips graze my neck, pressing a soft kiss before moving up, his hot breath whispering over the sensitive skin until our mouths become one, aligning in heated bliss. Our moans mingle in the hungry breaths between us, hearts reaching for the other's as we seek solitude in this moment.

"Austin," I breathe, reaching between us for his belt. "I need you. Please, right here, right now."

A growl shoves from his throat, his hands pushing beneath my dress, pulling my panties aside the same time I free him from the confines of his jeans. "Take me, baby. Take all of me."

My hand presses to the fogged-up window, leaving its mark as I slide down on him, deep and rushed. The joining is life altering, everything in my broken world suddenly righting itself like a stack of strewn dominos, one by one finding their place again as I find mine.

For the first time since my sister died, I feel warmth.

"You feel this, baby?" Austin groans, his fingers digging into my hips, branding my skin. "This right here, this is where you belong."

He's right, and I've never been more sure of it than I am in this moment. I know without a doubt that no matter where I go from here, whatever heartbreak I encounter, this is whom I will turn to.

This is where I will heal.

My forehead drops on his, my desolate tears slipping onto his face as he completes me like no one else ever could. "Don't stop," I choke out. "Please, don't ever stop."

Resolution burns deep within in his gaze, the promise reflecting back at me before he even speaks it. "Never, Zoey girl. You and me forever."

Love wraps around my heart, making that ache hurt a little less than it did before. Even though there is nothing that will ever fill the void of losing my sister, this man offers me a sanctuary I will never find anywhere else. As long as I have him, I'll always belong to someone.

With him, I am home.

CHAPTER TWENTY

Austin

A clicking noise pulls me from a deep sleep. Cracking an eye open, I find the view of an angel before me. A blonde-haired beauty wrapped in my white bed sheet, holding a camera as she snaps pictures of me. A woman I missed like fucking crazy this past week.

"What are you doing, Zoey girl?" My voice is gruff, thick with sleep.

She slides the camera away from her face, revealing blue eyes that hold less sadness and more of the woman I've fallen in love with. "Rediscovering my love of photography," she says with that sweet, soft voice of hers. "Thought I would start with the best scenery of all."

My cock stirs at the cute smile she gives. Gripping her hips, I lift her over to straddle me. "Then you should have started by standing in front of a mirror."

That smile I love so much inches further across her lips. It doesn't fully mask the pain in her eyes but it's a start. "Good one, Hawke."

The easy moment changes as I reach up, fingers grazing her cheek. "How are you feeling this morning?"

"Better since I got to wake up next to you."

Her answer has pride filling my chest. "Good, because it's how you will be waking up from now on."

She quirks a perfectly arched brow. "Are you asking me to move in with you, Hawke, or telling me?"

"Both." Before she can question that further, I push on. "This last week sucked without you, Zoey. I want you in my bed every night. Tell

125

me you want that, too."

"I do," she whispers. "I'd love nothing more than to wake up to you like this every morning."

"Then it's settled. We'll go get your stuff later today."

"In a hurry, are we?" she teases.

I shrug. "Just know what I want. No point in delaying it."

It's the truth. I've never felt the urge to cement my life with anyone else but her.

Her expression softens. "Me too."

"Good. Now that we've gotten that out of the way..." I roll her onto her back, dragging a laugh from her as I settle between her sweet thighs. "Let's move on to even better things." My hand grips the sheet between us, pulling it from her body as my lips drop to the exposed skin on her neck.

Moaning, she tilts her head, fingers gripping my shoulders. "I like where you're going with this, Hawke."

"Just wait, baby. You haven't seen anything yet." Before I can make good on that promise, there's a knock on my front door. My head lifts, eyes shifting in that direction. Slowly, I begin plotting the demise of whoever is on the other side.

"You were saying?" she says, barely containing a laugh.

Growling, I drop a hard kiss on her lips. "Hold that thought." Climbing from the bed, I pull my jeans on and walk out to answer the door.

On the other side are my two best friends.

"What the hell are you guys doing here?" I ask, unable to mask my annoyance at their terrible timing.

"Well aren't you Mr. Fucking Cheerful this morning." Cam enters without an invite, making himself comfortable at my kitchen island. "How about some breakfast? I'm famished."

I'm about to kick his ass out when Jake walks in next, his shoulders bunched with tension. "We need to talk."

Closing the door, I turn to them both, their grim expressions instantly putting me on alert. "What's going on?"

Before either can respond, Zoey walks out of my room. She carries her camera and is dressed in a pair of cutoff jean shorts and a pink tank top from the clothes she left here prior. Despite how good she looks, my mood sours even more when I realize we will not be picking up where we left off.

"So this is why you're so pissed off," Cam says, amusement laced in his voice as he speaks with no filter, as usual. "You're coveting a beautiful woman." Jumping off the kitchen stool, he walks over to Zoey, greeting her with a kiss on the cheek.

If he wasn't one of my best friends, I'd punch him in the mouth for putting his lips on my girl.

"Hey, Cam," she returns, accepting his gesture before giving Jake a small wave.

"How's it going, Zoey?"

She shrugs but answers honestly. "Just okay."

Jake nods in understanding. If anyone can grasp what she's going through right now, it's him. "Listen, we can come back," he says, his attention back on me. "We should have called first."

"No, please stay. It's fine." Zoey assures him, swinging her gaze my way. "Do what you need to do here. I'm going to go explore the property and test out the new camera. Meet up when you're done?"

I nod. "I'll come find you. Don't go far."

She gives me a mock salute. "Yes, sir, Lieutenant."

I grunt but the truth is, I'll take the sass over her sadness any day.

Chuckling, she blows me a kiss that Cam pretends to catch, making her laugh even harder.

Asshole.

Though, I can't deny I love that sound, even if he's the one to invoke it.

After one final wave, she walks out the door.

"Guess you guys patched things up," Cam remarks, opening his trap once again.

"There was nothing to patch up. She just needed some time. I gave it to her and now she's back."

"Whatever you say, *Lieutenant,*" he mocks.

I shoot him an annoyed look before turning to face Jake, my arms crossing over my chest. "What's going on?"

Within seconds the energy in the room shifts, and I quickly realize I'm not going to like this. "Cam found out something interesting about our rookie yesterday."

My curiosity piques, eyes shifting back to Cam, finding all prior amusement gone from his face.

"Remember that shift Rubin switched with Declan because of a family gathering?" he asks.

I nod.

"Well, turns out there never was a family gathering."

"How do you know that?"

"I ran into Clay at the gym last night," he says, talking about Rubin's older brother. The four of us graduated together. "We got on the topic of Declan's death and how Rubin has been handling it. He said he hasn't been himself since the fire, more stressed and agitated, even withdrawn. When I mentioned how the shift change must make it harder on him, he had no idea what I was talking about. Needless to say, by the time I was finished telling him, he was as confused as me."

I mull over the information, something feeling off. "Why would Rubin lie? It makes no sense."

Cam shrugs. "Maybe he has something to hide."

The suggestion triggers a memory, the back of my neck tingling as I recall finding him going through Declan's locker shortly after his death. I didn't think it was important before but maybe it was.

Tension mounts further when I share the information with them.

"Why didn't you say anything before?" Jake asks.

"Because he said he was looking for something that he lent to Declan. I didn't think he was fucking lying. This is Rubin we're talking about."

"I get it," Cam says, "but even if we put all this aside, I have to agree with Clay. Rubin hasn't been himself since Declan. Just look at how many times he's shown up late for shift in the last month."

He's right and it's not smart on his part. I've already given him a warning, next time it will be Cap, and when it comes to him, three strikes and you're out.

"Let's also not forget how skittish he was when the chief showed up the other night," he adds, making another good point. "He ran back into that station like his ass was on fire."

"Maybe, but arson?" I say. "I just don't see it. He's too...amateur."

"I agree with you there," Jake says. "But I still say we take this to Cap. He needs to know, Austin. Right now, with the escalation of these fires, we can't rule anything out."

I let go of a heavy breath and nod. "We'll talk to him next shift."

The last thing we need is more tension around the station but they're right, Cap needs to know about this. I just hope we're wrong and there is a very good explanation for all this because the thought that it could be one of our own, that it could be someone from our very station, leaves me sick to my stomach.

CHAPTER TWENTY-ONE

Zoey

Surrounded by nature, I take my time snapping photo after photo as I rediscover a passion I'd abandoned over time.

At first I wandered the property, feeling a little unsure as I trudged through the wet grass from the rain we had earlier. It was almost like I had forgotten how to do this, but it didn't take long before I found my love all over again.

It started with the sun casting a glow on the mountain peaks as it broke from the clouds. Then a squirrel on a branch eating an acorn. A bird's nest that had newborn baby birds. Discovery after discovery came and euphoria slipped over me, the burden on my heart easing with every shot I captured. Until time became nothing more than an afterthought.

One of the things I love most about photography is the ability to see things differently through a lens, experience them differently. Things that you wouldn't normally appreciate with the naked eye.

It reminds you just how big the world really is and that despite the catastrophes it can hold, the heartbreak it can bleed, somewhere within this madness we call life lies beauty.

It isn't until I come upon the creek that my feet falter and I remember the last time I was here.

With my sister and Austin.

The newfound peace I had just discovered shatters, pain threading through my hurting heart as I remember that day. It's so vivid that I'm thrust back into the memory, reliving it all over again.

Chrissy's stuttering laugh carries with the soft breeze, lighting up her entire being as Austin carries her down to the water, kneeling so she can touch it.

"Co-ld," she muses, smiling back at him.

"It is. Do you want to go for a swim?" he teases, pretending to throw her in the water.

She shrieks with laughter, clinging to his shirt.

Eventually, he walks her further down the bank, showing her the different rocks and a dam that was built before he moved in.

I snap pictures of them with my phone, my heart full as I watch the man I love carry my baby sister in his strong arms and show her the beautiful parts of Mother Nature. He doesn't complain or even break a sweat. By the smile on his face, I'd say he's enjoying it as much as Chrissy is. It's all I can do to contain the sheer joy I feel in this moment.

I end up picking a spot on the grass and empty out the picnic basket we packed before calling them over.

Austin situates Chrissy between my open legs, her back resting against my chest as I hug her close, then he takes the spot behind me, his arms coming around both my sister and me. It's the most perfect moment of my existence, one I decide I must capture.

Turning my phone to selfie mode, I hold it up, far enough to get all three of us in. "Everyone say cheese."

My sister's smile fills the screen while Austin turns his face, his lips pressing to my cheek. It's a moment that will not only be in a photo forever but also photographed on my heart for the rest of my life.

A bird chirps next to me, pulling me from the memory and bringing me back to my devastating reality. I find myself down on my knees, tears streaming down my face as my heart bleeds with longing, wishing I could have several more moments just like that one. All the times we were supposed to have but were stolen from us much too soon.

My breath shudders, agony slicing my chest as I feel myself being pulled back into grief. One moment, I'm lost in my despair, and then the next, everything changes.

The sun suddenly becomes brighter, dancing along my skin and calling my attention. Lifting my face, I gasp at what I find before me.

A rainbow.

A beautiful, unmistakable rainbow that lights up the entire sky, touching my soul like never before.

A kiss from heaven.

"Chrissy." Her name leaves my lips on the softest whisper, a feeling of unconditional love washing over me.

"Zoey!" Austin's worried voice breaks into the moment as he races forward, dropping down before me. He frames my tear stained cheeks between both his hands, his concerned eyes searching mine. "What's wrong? Are you hurt?"

I shake my head.

"What happened?"

"I…" I trail off, words rolling around in my head as I think of a way to explain this to him, but how do you explain something as extraordinary as this? How do you explain the unexplainable? "I think I'm going to be okay," I tell him instead.

Understanding flashes across his face before remorse fills it. "You will be, Zoey girl. I'll make sure of it." He pulls me into his arms, holding my fragile pieces together as we both look out at the rainbow, silence settling between us.

I snap a few pictures but know a photo will never bring this moment justice. Nothing can.

"I think she knew," I say softly, telling Austin something I haven't been able to admit. "I think Chrissy knew she was going to leave me."

His lips brush my temple in comfort. "Why do you say that?"

I shrug. "Just some of the things she said and did."

Over the last few weeks, I've replayed some of our last moments together. Remembering the night she touched my face, telling me she wanted me to be happy, it has knowledge filling my heart, one I haven't wanted to accept.

"I didn't want to believe it," I whisper. "I knew she was suffering but I still selfishly wanted her to stay."

"You love her, Zoey. There's nothing selfish in that."

Maybe he's right but I can't help but feel a sense of guilt, thinking she held on as long as she did only for me. She worried about me and wanted to make sure I was happy. She sacrificed for me too, probably more than I did for her. With every precious beat of my heart, that awareness spreads and it's something I won't take for granted, not anymore.

The last thought has me saying what I do next. "I'm going to sell the bar."

"Yeah?" he asks, a note of surprise in his voice.

I nod, though it wasn't until I just spoke those words that I realize just how confident I am in the decision. "As much as I appreciate all it has given me, it was always only meant as a means to support Chrissy. Now that she's gone it just doesn't feel right anymore. It's...lost its purpose," I add, remembering the words he said to me last night.

"Then sell it. Do what makes you happy, Zoey. I'll be here for whatever you decide."

I smile, my heart swelling with the love this man makes me feel. Turning in his arms, I look up into his handsome face. "You make me happy."

"Good because you're never getting rid of me." His warm brown eyes hold mine captive as his mouth descends, sealing this moment with a promise. It isn't long before we are shedding our clothes and making love under the sun, finding something beautiful amongst the pain.

CHAPTER TWENTY-TWO

Zoey

Friday afternoon, I walk into the bar to find Frank standing behind the counter, doing inventory before it opens for business.

His head lifts at my arrival, relief flashing in his dark eyes before disapproval takes over. "You're not working tonight."

His surly tone doesn't deter me in the least. I continue forward, my hands lifting in surrender. "Don't worry, I'm not here to work. I'm here to see you."

"Oh. Well in that case, get your ass over here and give me a hug."

A giggle escapes my mouth as he meets me halfway, embracing me while I give him a kiss on the cheek. His hands move to my shoulders as he steps back, his eyes assessing. "You're looking better, sweetheart. Still sad but better."

"Thanks. I'm trying."

"That's all we can do." He pulls out a bar stool, gesturing for me to sit. "Have a seat. Want something to drink?"

"No, thanks. I'm good."

He takes the chair to my right, turning to face me. "What's up?"

I open my mouth to speak what I came to say but then close it. No matter how many times I went over this in my head, I still find myself lost for words, feeling nervous for his reaction.

He cocks a brow, waiting patiently.

Squaring my shoulders, I decide to just blurt it out. "I'm going to sell the bar."

I wait for his surprise but it never comes. "I think that's a good idea."

Shock rolls through me, a frown taking over my face. "You do?"

He nods. "Your heart has never been in this place, not the way it should be."

My shoulders slump, guilt working its way into my chest. "Was I really that bad at hiding it?"

He shrugs. "What's there to hide? You ran this place with pride and worked your ass off for your sister. Nothing wrong with that."

Warmth invades my chest. This man may not have known me long but he gets me.

"I did and I appreciate all it's given me. It's just not where I'm meant to be anymore, ya know?"

"I get it, and as I said, I think it's the right decision."

"I'm glad to hear that because I want to ask you something."

"Oh?" He peers back at me, waiting for elaboration.

"Any chance you want to buy it from me?"

The surprise I expected earlier now flashes across his face. "Me?"

I nod. "This may not have been my dream job but the bar still means a lot to me and I want someone who will love it the way it deserves. I'm not looking to make money," I rush to assure him. "Not if you take it. I'd be willing to just hand over the loan as is."

He waves me away. "Don't worry about that. We'd make this fair for both of us. I just...I never thought about the possibility." He pauses, pondering it for only a minute. "I'll take it."

I sit up straighter, caught off guard by the quick response. "Really? You don't want to think about it more? Because you can."

"Nope. I'm making my decision now. I want it."

A sense of relief slips over me, the weight of the world lifting from my shoulders. "Then it's yours."

A grin stretches across his face, his hand lifting in the air. "Can you see it? Frank Lowery, bar owner," he says, an almost wistful sound to his voice. "Sounds good, don't it?"

I'm unable to hide my own smile. "It sounds wonderful."

Laughing, he jumps to his feet. "Come here, sweetheart."

Jumping off my stool, I walk into his arms, our hug lasting longer than our first one.

"Thanks for always being my friend, Frank," I murmur against his chest.

"I'll always be your friend, kid, and you will always have a place in this bar if you ever change your mind."

My heart swells as I realize just how lucky I am to have this man in my life. He's been more of a father to me than my own ever was. No matter where we go from here, I know he will always be a part of my life.

A loud bang suddenly sounds from the kitchen, pulling us apart.

"Is Tara here already?" I ask.

"Shouldn't be."

He heads toward the kitchen with me following close behind but when we enter we find it empty.

"Don't tell me we have damn mice. It'd be just my luck after buying this place."

I chuckle but it quickly trails off when a distinct odor suddenly fills the room. Something that smells oddly sweet. It's so overwhelming that it makes me nauseous.

My gaze swings to Frank. "Do you smell that?"

Confusion masks his expression seconds before a blast rocks the ground, throwing us off our feet. I land with jarring impact, my ears ringing with painful finality as the air gets shoved from my lungs. Fiery debris rains down upon us as the entire world crumbles, trapping us in darkness.

CHAPTER TWENTY-THREE

Austin

Cam, Jake, and I sit before the captain in his office, relaying the information we found out about Rubin. I hate to do this but the more I've thought about his deceit, the more concerned I've become. We deserve the truth about where he was that night and, as lieutenant, it's my job to get to the bottom of it, especially when this shift change helped cause the death of one of my men.

"This is a serious accusation, you all understand that, right?"

"No one is accusing him yet, Cap," I respond carefully. "We just want the truth. Clearly he lied about where he was that night, and I want to know why."

"Same," Cam says, cutting in. "As much as I hate to entertain this idea, you have to admit it's a little unnerving, especially when Austin caught him going through Declan's locker only days after his death."

Cap nods. "It is but that doesn't make him a criminal. He and Declan were close. It makes no sense why he would put him in harm's way, or anyone for that matter." His eyes move to Jake for the first time since this meeting. "What's your take on all this? I know you've been discussing things with Hamilton."

Jake shrugs. "Honestly, I don't know. The more I think about it, the more I feel he doesn't fit the profile but I do agree that these instances are more than suspicious. I also think it's time we start considering that this could be personal."

"What makes you say that?" Cap asks, looking more than intrigued by his statement.

"These fires keep happening in our jurisdiction. He could strike anywhere at any time. Yet he chooses our territory. First two I thought was coincidental but after this last one…" He tugs at the back of his neck. "I don't know, Cap. Something doesn't feel right. Call it a gut feeling."

His gut feelings are usually pretty accurate. It's one of the reasons I trust him to have my back, but if I'm being honest, I have considered this option, too. I think we all have. The question though is, why? What would someone have against us or this station, especially Rubin.

"Look, Cap," I speak up again. "Considering the circumstances, I think we at least have the right to question Marks about this, especially since no one is any closer to uncovering the arsonist."

He nods. "All right but we tread carefully. Last thing I need is the board breathing down my neck about unfair accusations. Besides, there could be a perfectly good explanation for all of this."

"True," Cam says. "But now begs the question, where is he?" He gestures to the clock. "Rookie is running twenty minutes late, something that seems to be a habit lately, and if you ask me, it's not helping his case."

As if the question summons him, Rubin comes running into the station, sweat covering his skin. He sends us a frantic wave through the glass as he passes by the office. "Sorry, Cap. Got stuck in traffic. It won't happen again."

Captain's lips press together in a thin line, his displeasure evident.

Before we have a chance to talk about how to approach this, the alarm rings with a call, sending us in motion. Our chairs scrape across the floor as we bolt from Cap's office, Rubin following after dropping his bag in the hallway.

The entire station is called out, right down to truck seventeen, the ambulance, and my rescue squad. The radio rattles off the details as we pull on our gear. When I hear there's been an explosion, unease settles in my gut, fearing the arsonist has struck again. Soon though, that feeling turns into something else, something incomprehensible when the address is relayed.

Zoey!

Terror thrashes through my veins, making my blood run cold. Cam's and Jake's eyes meet mine, their thoughts reflecting my worst fear.

"Move out now!" The order barely makes its way past my throat as urgency propels me into the passenger seat, the rest of my team jumping into the back.

Sirens pierce the air as Carl pulls away, following truck seventeen while Cap pulls out in line behind us.

I reach for my cellphone and dial Zoey, praying like hell she hasn't left yet. The little hope I cling to evaporates when I get her voicemail.

"Fuck!" I throw my phone, fear crashing down on me. "I think she's there." Every word is choked out past the panic threatening to claim me.

Jake's hand lands on my shoulder from the backseat. "Take it easy, man. If she is, we'll get her."

"He's right, Lieutenant. We got this."

My attention darts to Rubin as he speaks, tension mounting in my body as I think about his late arrival.

Silence fills the truck, my narrowed eyes making him shift in his seat.

"Hawke!" Cap's voice crackles from the radio, breaking the tension.

Clearing my tight throat, I hit the button on my mic. "Yeah."

"Is Zoey there right now?"

I swallow thickly, eyes briefly closing as my mind strays to the unthinkable. "I believe so, sir."

"I want you to stay out with me. Let the others—"

"No!" I cut him off before he can go further. "Don't do this to me, Cap. I have too much at stake."

"That's exactly why you shouldn't go in," he bellows.

"No one will fight for her like I will, sir, and we both know it." As much as I trust Cam and Jake, no one's best will be as good as mine.

"I've never let you down before. Give me this chance."

Silence fills the line and I pray he comes to his senses, because the last thing I want is to disobey orders from my captain, but if that's what it comes down to, I will. Nothing will stop me from going in to find her, no matter what destruction awaits us.

"We'll have his back, Cap," Jake adds, backing me up.

The radio eventually crackles. "Fine, but I'm calling the shots for this one. You follow my orders. Do you understand?"

"Yes, sir." I make the promise but know it's weak because no order will come before Zoey's life.

Thick gray smoke covers the sky the closer we get to our destination, making the knot in my stomach tighten.

Carl slams on the brakes, laying on the horn as we move into heavy traffic.

"Come on, Carl. Find an alternate route."

"I'm trying, Lieutenant." His wheel spins as he weaves in and out of the stropped vehicles, turning down a back alley.

I fight to possess a semblance of calm, my patience nonexistent as my mind runs with worst-case scenarios.

Because of the traffic jam we were stuck in, police and ambulance are already controlling the scene when we pull up. The sight that I'm met with has a newfound fear fisting my chest.

"Jesus," Cam breathes out the one word, jumping out of the truck behind me.

Injured people line the sidewalks, paramedics assessing them within the chunks of scattered concrete and debris. The bar is barely left standing, most of it consisting of rubble and smoke.

This is different than the others, the flames barely existent but destruction more severe, making me wonder if anyone could even survive this. The thought is enough to ruin me.

Regardless of the differences, there is no mistaking the sweet odor that fills my nostrils. My jaw locks with the knowledge that the bastard has struck again, but this time it was on precious ground. This time threatens to take my whole world down with its devastation.

Cap nods over at me, expression solemn as he gives me the go-ahead before shouting orders to truck seventeen.

With a quick assessment from my vantage point, I see most entrances are blocked. "We're going in through the east side," I tell Cam and Jake, a sudden calmness slipping over me, despite the chaos roaring in my veins. "We'll assess more from the inside."

"Copy." Cam reaches for the sledgehammer we'll need to break through the concrete while Jake and I slip on our oxygen tanks.

"Where do you want me, Lieutenant?" Rubin asks, sounding too eager for my liking.

I fight to rein in my suspicion, knowing now is not the time. "You be ready with any tools we call for."

"Come on, Lieutenant. Let me come with you. I wanna be where the action is this time."

My control snaps, hand shooting out as I shove him up against the truck. I lean close, getting into his face. "You stay the fuck out of my way and follow orders. Do you hear me? You have enough to answer for."

Shock registers on his face before anger tightens his features but he's smart enough to heed the order. "Yes, sir."

I shove away from him and head in for the rescue. My two best friends fall in step next to me, all of us masking up, determination fueling each stride we take. I have only one purpose and it comes at no cost.

I will risk it all to save her, even if it means giving my own life.

CHAPTER TWENTY-FOUR

Zoey

Fire rages in my lungs, eyes burning even more as I cough and sputter through the billowing smoke. I drag myself to my knees, my entire body screaming in protest.

Warmth drips down my face next, spilling onto the ground. Lifting my hand, I quickly realize it's blood, the color crimson staining my fingertips. A whimper of fear breaches my lips as I try to comprehend what's happened.

"Frank!" His name shoves from my dry throat, rasping through the air. "Frank, can you hear me?"

"Over here."

Hope inflates my chest when I hear his gruff voice. I wave the dust out of my face, trying to see through the destruction as I feel my way over to him. It isn't long before I find him, barely making out his form through all the debris.

"Thank God. Are you all right?"

"I'm pinned." Pain laces his voice, straining his words.

My gaze coasts down his body, terror lodging in my throat when I find the heavy steel cooler on his legs. "Do you think you can shift enough for me to drag you out?" I ask, knowing there is no way I'll be able to move it.

He shakes his head, expression pinched in agony.

"Okay, it's going to be okay." The assurance is just as much for myself as it is for him, panic threatening to pull me under.

I scan our surroundings, hoping to find a way to get help, but it doesn't take me long to realize just how much trouble we're in. Buried within the walls of destruction, the broken concrete and debris block any form of escape.

I climb to my feet, adrenaline and desperation pushing me past the pain screaming through my body. "Wait here."

"Kinda hard for me to go anywhere, sweetheart."

If I had it in me to laugh right now I would, but there is nothing funny about this. I step over the demolished earth, dodging broken glass and rubble. A severed wire sticks out from the wall, sparks flying from the end of it, sending me in the opposite direction.

Once I come up to a wall of broken concrete, I pull at the large chunks, using all the strength I possess. I pull at it so hard that the tips of my fingers begin to bleed. A cry of frustration leaves me, my fist hitting the rock when I make no progress.

"Help! Can anyone hear me? We're trapped!" Pain rattles my head as I call for rescue, but I shove it aside and continue calling for help. Unfortunately, nothing but silence greets my ears.

Defeat slips over me, drowning what little hope I had. Tears prick my eyes but I blink them back, knowing crying won't help anything right now.

When Frank lets out an agonized groan, I walk back over, kneeling next to him. "Do you happen to have your cellphone on you?"

I don't even want to think where mine could be right now.

"In my left pocket," he answers, voice weak.

I pat down the side of his body, frantically reaching inside of his pocket, and it causes another painful grunt.

"Easy there, sweetheart. This isn't a fishing expedition."

This time, a chuckle does escape me but it's short-lived, trailing into a desperate sob. "Now is not the time to be making jokes, Frank."

"Take a breath, darlin'. It'll be okay. Someone will come for us."

If they know we are somewhere in this wreckage. My biggest fear is we're buried too deep for anyone to find us. By the time they do, it could be too late. I let that terrifying thought trail off and dial 9-1-1.

It's to no avail, reception nonexistent.

"Shit!" The cellphone drops in my lap, my dread growing with every passing second. I notice Frank's head lull to the side and realize he's losing consciousness. "No, no, no. Frank, don't fall asleep. Please. Stay with me. I can't do this on my own."

"I'm with ya, kid. Just resting my eyes." He breaks into a coughing fit, furthering my concern.

I pull my thin sweater off my shoulders. "Here. Use this." I cover his mouth with it, using it as a filter against the dirty air.

"No, you," he says, pushing it away.

"I'm fine right now. You need it more than I do." Refusing to argue, I cover his face then lift his head to prop it on my lap as I settle in behind him. "Does this help or make it worse?"

"As long as you're with me, sweetheart, it helps."

My heart swells, tears welling in my eyes again. "I won't leave your side, Frank."

"And I won't leave yours." His hand grasps mine, squeezing tight. "I couldn't even if I wanted to."

A watery laugh escapes me as I shake my head, but I don't scold him for his misplaced humor. Not this time.

I continue to try his phone, praying for a single bar, but remain unsuccessful. Every passing minute my concern grows, fearing no one will be able to find us in the midst of this destruction.

My thoughts stray to Austin, heart breaking at the thought of never seeing him again. When my sister died, a part of me wanted to be with her, no matter where that was, but as I face death now, I know that's not where I'm meant to be. I still have too much to live for. So much to do with Austin. I'm not ready to lose that.

"You hanging in there, Frank?"

"I'm here," he wheezes. "I don't know about you but I'm damn hungry. I skipped lunch."

This man and his jokes.

With a smile, I open my mouth to toss out the irony of us being in the kitchen when the sparking wire suddenly stops flailing, losing its power. I sit up straighter, swearing I hear something in the distance.

"Seriously. I could really go for—"

"Shh," I cut him off. "Do you hear that?"

"Hear what?"

Silence fills the span of a second just before some rubble falls from the wall. "Fire department, anyone here?"

"That!" I cry on a laugh, praising the Lord for the blessed interruption.

"Zoey, can you hear me?"

Austin's voice sends relief hurdling through my chest. "Yes, we're in here," I yell, breaking into a coughing fit as I suck in dust-filled air. "Please hurry. Frank is trapped."

The sound of steel banging against concrete penetrates the heavy air before more rubble and rock fall away, leaving a small hole to start forming. I squint at the flashlight shining in, covering my eyes.

"I see them," someone relays, sounding a lot like Jake.

I'd be happy to see anyone right now but I can't deny just how much more grateful I am that it's the three of them.

"Hold on, baby. Just a little more and we will be in there. Whatever you do, stay where you are."

I nod, even though he can't see me. "Hang in there, Frank. They're coming."

It isn't long before the hole is big enough for them to fit through, all three of them rushing in with a stretcher.

Austin comes to my side while the other two drop down by Frank.

"Look at me." His hands cup my face, eyes filled with panic. "You okay?"

"I am now."

A heavy breath escapes him as he pulls me into his arms. "Jesus, I was so fucking scared."

"Me too," I confess, hugging him just as tightly. "I have no idea what happened. The blast came out of nowhere and…" I break into a coughing spell, taking in too much air as I frantically try to deliver our encounter.

"Easy, baby. Don't talk." He slips off his mask and holds it over my face. "Deep breaths."

I do as he instructs, the clean air a welcome reprieve to my burning lungs.

"How's it going, Frank?" Cam greets him, assessing his pinned situation.

"Been better," he grunts.

"Well next time you get hungry don't get so excited," he tosses back, making Jake chuckle next to him.

"Hardy fucking har, get this damn thing off me."

Obviously, he's not in the joking mood anymore.

"Can you feel your legs?" Austin asks him, checking his vitals.

"What the hell do you think? Hell no, this damn thing weighs a ton."

A smirk twitches Austin's lips before he looks up at the other two. "He'll be okay. Let's try the airbags first. If they don't work, we'll get Marks to bring in the jaws."

Small deflated bags are placed underneath the cooler before they are blown up, lifting the heavy appliance just enough for them to get Frank on the stretcher and out from beneath it.

Despite his earlier comment about not being able to feel his legs, he groans, the painful sound making me wince.

Austin presses the mic on his jacket. "Cap, we have them. We'll be out soon, have medics waiting."

"Copy."

Austin helps me to my feet while the other two lift the stretcher. Jake backs over the destruction, leaving Cam at the head of it. As they walk for the makeshift entrance, I suddenly feel my feet come out from under me, a gasp of surprise fleeing past my lips.

"Easy, Zoey girl. I got you." Austin's soothing voice whispers in my ear, his strong arms settling me against his broad chest.

"I can walk," I assure him. As much as I love being in his arms, I don't want to make this harder on him.

"Yeah, I know, but right now I need to feel you breathing against me."

I gaze back into his dirty smudged face, love filling my heart like never before.

The mask slides away from my face as he leans in, his lips moving for mine. I wait with bated breath, needing to feel the connection more than ever.

"Zoey, where are ya?" Frank attempts to shout from his prone position ahead of us, breaking up our reunion. "You okay back there?"

"Right behind you, Frank," I return, smiling back at Austin sheepishly.

"Good, because we need to talk about what kind of insurance you have on this place."

Chuckling, I rest my head on Austin's shoulder as he carries me to safety, thanking God we escaped with our lives and Frank didn't lose his sense of humor after all.

CHAPTER TWENTY-FIVE

Austin

Tensions run high in the conference room, Rubin sitting before the captain and I as we question where he was the night of the warehouse fire that killed Declan.

It's all I can do to remain calm and professional because, right now, *professional* is the last thing I feel. The explosion was two days ago. Two days ago I almost lost the woman I love all because some fucking pyromaniac has an agenda. It's time for answers and I intend to get them, starting with our prime suspect.

"I already told you guys. I had a family dinner that night."

That ever-present rage continues to build inside of me as he blatantly lies straight to our faces again.

"Well, you see, Rubin, this is the problem." Cap starts calmly. "Cam saw your brother the other night at the gym and he said there was no family dinner."

His facade slips. He swallows hard, shifting in his seat as he realizes he's been busted.

"Where were you, Marks?" I ask, my suspicion unmistakable.

"I was taking care of something, okay? It's private." His flippant response has my anger exploding to the surface.

My hands slam down on the table before him, making him jump. "You're riding a thin fucking line here. Now is not the time for cryptic answers. Declan is dead from that shift change and my girl was almost killed two days ago, conveniently the same time you showed up late for your shift. If I were you, I'd start talking, really fucking quick."

"Wait a second," he says, holding up a hand. "You guys think I'm the one starting these fires?"

"We just need some clarification," Cap explains. "You haven't been honest with us about the shift you switched with Declan. You've also been late too many times to count, and like Austin has mentioned, coincidentally the fire started yesterday in your absence."

"I didn't do it. I swear!"

"Then tell us where you were the night Declan died," I say, cutting back in. "We're willing to give you the benefit of the doubt here, Marks, but give us something to go on. Anything."

I hold onto the little bit of hope I have left, praying he has some sort of explanation for all this. The last thing I want is for him to be responsible, but as of right now, there's too many unanswered questions with him.

"I can't," he murmurs. "I'm sorry."

My hands fist at my sides as I restrain myself from beating the truth out of him.

"Then you leave me no choice," Cap says regretfully. "Under the circumstances, I'm going to have to suspend you until further notice, pending a full investigation."

He jumps to his feet, chair knocking over in his haste. "This is bullshit. I'd never hurt anyone, especially Declan. He was my best fucking friend!"

"Stand down, Marks," Cap orders before I can. "You've made your choice, now I've made mine. Go clean out your locker."

He kicks the knocked-over chair and storms out of the office.

Cam and Jake walk in after his angry departure, Cam blowing out a low whistle at the tipped over chair. "I'm guessing it didn't go well."

"No," I answer grimly. "He lied again about where he was and refused to give us the truth."

"I had to suspend him," Cap adds, guilt hanging in his voice.

"You did the right thing, Cap," Cam assures him.

He nods but you can see how hard the decision was on him.

"I still think we need to be open to the idea that this might not be him," Jake says. "After yesterday's fire it's safe to say this is more than a little personal."

"Agreed," I say, feeling the knowledge burning in my mind and heart. "This isn't just some asshole wreaking havoc on our town. He's targeting this station specifically and Zoey got caught in the crossfire." Just speaking it has rage searing my veins all over again. "If it's not Rubin we need to find out who and soon or there is no telling who's next."

Cap lets go of a weary breath, running a hand down his tired face. "I'll talk to arson. In the meantime, you guys watch your backs. Every call is always handled with care but even more so now. Understand?"

"Yes, sir."

After we're dismissed, we leave his office, Cam speaking again once we enter the hallway. "If you ask me, I think it's time we do some hunting of our own. I'm tired of waiting to see what this sick fuck will do next."

"Same," Jake adds, voice hard. "I know Cap wants Roper to handle this but I don't trust him. It's time we start doing some investigating of our own."

I nod my agreement. No more waiting. We need to catch this fucker and when we do, he will pay for ever trying to hurt what's mine.

CHAPTER TWENTY-SIX

The night is ablaze with red, yellow, and orange lighting up the dark sky as I watch the structure disintegrate before me. Flames crackle and roar, licking the empty window frames. They reach for me like the devil himself, calling on my dark soul as they try pulling me into the depths of hell. While the heat is strong, nothing compares to the rage burning in my heart.

A smile claims my lips, satisfaction rolling through me as I think about everything I still have planned. They haven't seen anything yet.

By the time I am done, they will all bleed the same pain and betrayal they have bestowed upon me.

EPILOGUE

Zoey

S unlight cascades through the broken clouds as I trek across the property carrying my camera and the mysterious map that was left next to me in bed.

I woke up this morning, reaching for the warm body I'm used to feeling wrapped around me only to find this piece of paper with specific instructions and a map to follow.

My mind has run rampant with all sorts of scenarios as to what he could be up to, all of them making my heart dance in my chest. Beautiful feelings that are no longer foreign to me since he came into my life.

A lot has happened since the fire, life changing things that have me feeling thankful every day for the second chance I've been given.

It started with a contract I was offered from National Geographic. Thanks to Austin, who sent in some of my work without my knowledge, not only did they show interest and purchase the rainbow photograph I took all those weeks ago right here on this very property, they also offered me a three-year contract to work for them.

It's always been a dream of mine, and thanks to Austin, he made it come true. I'll be taking pictures within this beautiful state and all over the world. My very first travel destination is Fiji and Austin gets to come with me. We leave next week, and I can't wait to explore it with him.

It will be good for us to get away from the craziness for a little while. Things at work for him have been strained, to say the least. They are no closer to uncovering the identity of the arsonist who is terrorizing our community. From what Austin has told me, they don't even have enough evidence for the only suspect they have. It's scary and I worry about his safety constantly.

Aside from that, things are slowly falling into place. Thanks to the insurance money, Frank has been able to rebuild the bar. Austin has been giving him a hand when he has free time, and I know he will make the new place a success. I couldn't be happier for him and I've promised to be his first customer.

All of the wonderful things happening in my life have helped ease the pain of losing my sister. I'll always miss her, always long for her, that will never change, but every day that ache gets a little less and most of it is thanks to the man who owns my heart.

I come up to my first point marked on the map, a confused frown forming on my face when I find a shot glass resting on a folded piece of paper. I snap a picture of it first, wanting to photograph this little mission he has me on, then bend down and pick it up. Opening the folded piece of paper, it reads:

One night I walked into a bar for a drink with my hockey team, never knowing I'd come face-to-face with an angel. From there, it began.

An unmistakable smile claims my lips, butterflies flocking in my tummy as I continue to the second point of interest, eager to see what I will find next.

Laughter rattles my chest when I recognize the paddle from the auction I used to bid on him with a hundred-dollar bill tied to the handle. After snapping a photo, I pick it up along with the note:

You finally took a chance on me and it was the best night of my existence. I would have spent another thousand dollars for a single night with you and I'll spend even more for a lifetime.

My breath catches at the written words, a sliver of hope igniting in my chest at what this all could be leading up to. Looking down at the map, I continue to the next checkpoint, not missing the fact that it's taking me to my favorite place on the property.

The creek.

A familiar blanket is spread out, the same one we made love on that first night in front of the fire. A picnic basket rests on it along with a wrapped gift and two flowers, a daffodil and a pink lily. There's no mistaking whom the pink one represents.

Emotion burns my throat, sharpening the ache that will always remain in my heart. After snapping the picture, I take a spot on the soft blanket and pick up both flowers, bringing them to my nose for a smell. The sweet scent recovers the memory of the day he surprised us at the hospital.

A note tells me to open the wrapped gift first. Picking it up, I bring it on my lap and peel away the paper to find a framed photo. It's the selfie I took of the three of us in this very spot. One of the last moments we were all together before her death.

The tears I've been holding back begin to tumble down my cheek as I hold the photo close to my heart. My face tilts up to the sun, letting the warmth of it mask the love and loss I feel in this moment.

Once I gain a measure of control, I open the letter that comes with it.

She may not be here with us now but it doesn't change the fact that she will be a part of our lives forever. I promised the both of you that I would give you everything you ever wanted and I'm starting right now.

Open the picnic basket.

Putting the letter down, I swipe at my tears then flip open the top of the basket. What I find has a gasp fleeing me. "Oh my goodness. Who are you?"

Reaching inside, I pull out the cutest yellow lab puppy, his chubby belly squirming in my hands excitedly.

"Well aren't you just the sweetest little thing." I bring him into my chest and look down at his collar; the name on his dog tag has a small sob breaching my lips.

Gus.

I hug the dog close, crying as I hold a dream my sister and I had together for as long as I can remember. I'm yanked from the emotional moment when his wet nose tickles my face, making me laugh.

"You like kisses? Me too." I press my lips to the top of his nose, loving his puppy scent.

"Hey. Those kisses are supposed to be for me."

The deep, amused voice has my head snapping up. My heart turns over in my chest when I find the man responsible for all this. A sexy smirk rests on his face as he walks toward me, his long gait as sure and confident as ever.

He comes to a stop in front of me, looking proud as he gazes down at me.

"What have you done, Austin Hawke?" I sniffle, finding it hard to find the words I'm feeling in this moment.

"Just trying to make you mine forever."

His response turns me into a blubbering mess. "I can't believe you did all this."

He drops down to both knees before me, brushing my hair out of my face. "I'd do anything for you, Zoey girl, and if you give me the chance, I promise to make every single dream you ever have come true."

There's no stopping the flow of tears no matter how much I try. They slip down my cheeks, making Gus's yellow fur golden until he wiggles out of my arms and onto the grass.

Austin leans in, pressing his lips to my wet cheek, erasing the tears one by one just like he erases the pain in my heart. His mouth trails to my ear, making me wait with bated breath for what he will say next.

"Marry me, Zoey."

Even though I expected the words, they still change my entire life, solidifying my biggest dream of all.

To be his forever.

I lift my hand to his jaw, holding him close. "Yes."

Taking my left hand in his, he slides a stunning white gold ring onto my finger, the single solitaire perfectly fitting, but it's the two smaller pink stones on either side, which represents my sister, that takes my breath away.

"It's perfect," I whisper.

"A perfect ring for a perfect girl."

I wrap my arms around his neck. "Thank you," I cry. "Thank you for loving me, for saving me, but mostly, thank you for loving my sister and making her a part of this moment. I feel her here with us so much right now."

His arms curl around my waist, bringing me in even closer. "She'll always be with us, Zoey, and together we're going to live this life for her, too."

His words settle over me, burrowing into my heart. Pulling back, our eyes hold for two solid beats before our mouths become one, the soul-shattering kiss a promise of forever.

Groaning, he pulls me over to straddle him. My knees rest on either side of his hips while his hands cup my bottom, bringing me snug against his erection. "Always so fucking sweet, Zoey girl."

My fingers drive into his hair, every breath precious and urgent as we lose ourselves in one another.

The beautiful connection is broken up quickly though by a cold, wet nose as Gus wiggles himself between us. I pull back, sliding off his lap with a laugh as the small pup dances around, wanting to play.

"Hey," Austin scolds, lifting the tiny pup in the air. "You're seriously cockblocking me right now, dog."

My heart warms when he licks Austin's cheek in response before jumping into my arms.

"Awe, don't be too upset with him, Hawke," I coo, holding the puppy close to my heart. "We have our whole lives to make up for it."

Deep, dark eyes peer into mine, his hand reaching out to caress my cheek. "Yeah, we do, and I promise, Zoey, I'll always make you happy."

I have no doubt he will because he's already made me the happiest woman in the world, something I didn't think I'd ever feel again without my sister.

"Come on." He climbs to his feet, offering me his hand. "Let's take the little cockblocker for a walk."

Smiling, I allow him to pull me up, our fingers linking as we walk hand in hand next to the creek, watching as Gus plays in the water.

This moment is a promise of the future that I always dreamed about and I silently vow to live it for Chrissy. To never take a single day for granted and to love this man with everything I am.

Turn the page for a letter from the author...

Dear reader,

I hope you enjoyed the first book in my Men of Courage series. There is still so much to come and I can't wait to share more of these characters with you. Cam's book is second and Jake's will be the third and final story.

It is best to follow me on social media to keep up-to-date with what's to come next or my website www.authorkclynn.com where you can also read sneak peeks and short stories of previous written characters.

If you are a new reader to me, please feel free to check out my Men of Honor series. The first book *Fighting Temptation* is free on all platforms.

You can also turn the page to read the first chapter of *Sweet Haven,* Sam and Jase's book which is where we first met these fabulous characters. It is available now on all platforms.

Until next time,
K.C. Lynn

SWEET HAVEN
CHAPTER 1

Sam

Music vibrates beneath my feet as I head up to the bar with my tray in hand. "I need three Coronas, two Jack and Cokes, and a screwdriver for table seven," I tell my friend, Zoey, who's behind the counter.

"Got it." Lining up three glasses she begins filling the order. "I can't thank you enough, Sam, for bailing me out once again. Finding reliable help nowadays seems impossible, especially on a Friday night."

I smile back at her, feeling bad about how much trouble she's had finding good servers. Zoey is one of my best friends and owns Overtime, a successful sports bar here in Silver Creek. Anytime I can help her out I do, especially since the hours don't conflict with my day job. It also keeps me busy and my mind off of things. Things I don't like to think about.

"You know I'm happy to help whenever I can. It's not like my Friday nights are ever eventful."

She chuckles, knowing it's true. "Well, thank God for that or I would have been in one hell of a bind tonight. It's going to be hard to find backup when you leave me for good," she adds, speaking of my upcoming move to Charleston. Her smile dims as she places the first two drinks on my tray. "You know I'm going to miss the hell out of you, right?"

"I'll miss you, too," I confess, my throat beginning to feel tight. "But we still have three more months together. I promise to come visit and you can come see me, too."

"I know, but it won't be the same." She pops the caps off three Coronas before putting them down in front of me and reaching for the limes nearby. "The first thing I want you to do when you get there is go to your brother's gym and find yourself a sexy fighter. If you find two then send one my way."

"Yeah right, you know how Sawyer is. The last place I'll ever find a date will be at his gym."

"Well, he's going to have to get over the whole protective big brother thing. It's time you got back on the dating train, Sam. Now that the two-timing asshole is out of the picture."

My stomach knots at the mention of Grant.

Zoey senses the reaction. "Sorry, I didn't mean to bring him up."

I shake my head. "Don't be. It's fine."

Actually, it's not fine. Nothing to do with Grant was ever fine. If I could go back and change the seven months I foolishly gave him then I would. But I can't. All I can do is move on and never let myself stoop that low again. Being with my family again will help. I've missed them so much.

Shoving my thoughts aside, I flash Zoey my perfected fake smile before turning back to the packed bar to deliver my order. It really is a great place with booths and high-top tables littering the worn hardwood floors, creating a maze of sports enthusiasts, eager to catch whatever sporting event is on for the evening. Most local sports teams come in to either celebrate their victory or drown their sorrows.

As I place each drink in front of the waiting patrons, I feel a crowd at my back as people take the table behind me. I spin around to greet them with a bright smile that dies when my gaze collides with a pair of sexy chocolate brown eyes that girls drop their panties for in a heartbeat.

Jase Crawford, my brother's sworn enemy.

His gaze blatantly sweeps down my body, making my skin tingle before slowly climbing back up to my face. I stand tall, refusing to shift under his scrutiny, knowing that's exactly what he wants. A slight smirk plays at the edge of his full lips, but there's no denying the hint of hostility in his eyes as he stares back at me.

The sexy bastard.

No, not sexy. He's just a bastard.

Well, maybe he's a little sexy…or a lot. But definitely more bastard than sexy.

Frustrated with my internal debate, I shift my gaze away from his and focus on the rest of the group. My smile returns when I see a few of the guys he's with are Jake Ryan, Cam Phillips, and Austin Hawke. They work at the fire station with him and also happen to be childhood friends of Sawyer's.

"Well, if it isn't little Evans," Cam boasts, being the first to greet me.

"Hey, guys. Good to see you."

"You, too," Austin says. "How are things?"

"Good thanks, and you?"

He shrugs. "Can't complain. How about your brother? It's been a while since we spoke."

"He's doing great. Living the dream down in Charleston with his beautiful family. He even coached my nephew's first year of hockey last season. My dad swears he's a natural and the NHL's next legend," I relay with a proud smile.

There's a grunt to my left, interrupting our conversation.

Twisting my head, I glare at those mesmerizing brown eyes. "You have something to say, Crawford?"

If he makes one rude comment about my family, I'll mess up that pretty face of his.

"Nope, I've got nothing," he answers with an infuriating smirk.

That's what I thought.

I turn to dismiss him when he speaks again. "However, I would like a drink whenever you're done bragging about your *perfect* family."

My fists clench at my sides as I get the urge to slap the smug look off his sexy face. Choosing to ignore him, I return my attention back to

Austin and find his eyes lit with amusement.

"What can I get you, Austin?"

With a chuckle, he gives me his order.

I move to Cam next, then Jake, making my way around the table to everyone except Jase. Once I have their orders, it's only then that I acknowledge him.

"You?" I ask, keeping my eyes averted. If I look at him, I could end up being arrested for bodily harm...

Don't think about his body, Sam.

"Well, thanks for finally asking me, Peaches."

My teeth grind at the nickname. He started calling me that the last few times I've run into him, but I have no idea why. It drives me crazy.

"I'll take a bottle of Bud."

When I start away he gently snags my wrist, stopping me in my tracks. His touch ignites an inferno throughout my entire body that burns from my head right down to the tips of my pink painted toenails. I drop my gaze where his fingers sear my skin before meeting his eyes, getting lost in the deep dark irises.

"And while you're at it, fetch me a menu."

I snap back into myself at his condescending tone, narrowing my eyes in anger.

Oh, I'll fetch him something all right.

Yanking my hand back, I head to the bar, slamming my tray down with a resounding smack.

Zoey looks up at me from where she makes a Caesar, her brows arched. "You all right?"

"I'm fine, why?" I grind out.

"Because your cheeks are flushed and you look like you're about to rip someone's head off."

"I am."

"Who?"

I shake my head. "Don't worry about it."

Concern pinches her expression. "If someone is giving you problems, Sam, just say the word and his ass is gone."

"No, it's fine," I assure her. "It's just Jase Crawford. That man drives me crazy."

She looks over my shoulder with a smile. "Ah, the sexy fire boys are in the house." Her fingers dance in the air as she gives them all a wave before bringing her attention back to me. "What happened with Jase?"

"He pushes every single one of my buttons."

"I wish he would push mine, especially the one between my legs."

As irritated as I am, I can't help but laugh. By the smile she gives me it's clear that was her intention.

"Don't ever let him hear you say that. He doesn't need his ego fed."

"True, but you have to admit he's hot enough to be a little arrogant. They all are."

"Hey, whose side are you on here?" I ask defensively.

"Yours. Always yours, but there shouldn't be any sides with the two of you, Sam. The problem is between him and Sawyer. It always has been."

"Exactly. He hates my brother so of course that affects me, too. And let's not forget our fathers can't stand to be around each other either."

Though, I've never understood why.

"Okay. I get it. I do," she says. "I can assign Tara to their table. I'm sure she'll have no problem serving a group of sexy firefighters."

"No!" I reject her offer immediately. "I'm not going to give him the satisfaction. I can handle him."

"You sure?"

"Absolutely."

She shrugs. "Okay, let me know if you change your mind."

"I will. Thanks."

Relaying their order to her, I wait while she fills the drinks. When the sound of laughter cuts through the steady noise of the bar, I glance behind me and see it's coming from their table. Unable to stop myself, my eyes immediately lock with Jase's. He gives me a cocky wink that has my blood heating to a dangerous temperature.

Turning back around, my eyes land on the bottle of Tabasco next to Zoey. A smile dances across my lips as an idea forms. "Pass me that, will ya?"

"What?" she asks, bringing her attention up to me.

I gesture to the sauce next to her. "That."

Once she hands it to me, I unscrew the top and tap a few drops into the bottle of Budweiser before soaking the rim with it.

"What the hell are you doing?"

"Fighting fire with fire," I tell her, feeling my smile spread.

"Oh shit. I don't think that's a good idea."

"Don't worry about it. It's just a little hot sauce. No harm. No foul."

She shakes her head but a chuckle escapes her. "Fine, but you're on your own with this one."

"Don't worry. I can handle it," I promise before pointing over her shoulder. "I need a menu too, please."

After she passes me one, I slide it under my arm then lift my tray and head back over to their table. My smile is radiant as I stop beside Jase first. I place his beer down in front of him then take the thin booklet from under my arm.

"Your menu," I announce, slapping it against his chest with as much force as I can without losing my tray of drinks.

He flashes me those dimples of his that girls swoon over. "Why thanks, Peaches."

"No problem, *sugar plum*," I toss back, making him and everyone else at the table chuckle.

We'll see how funny he thinks it is a minute from now.

I keep him in sight as I deliver the rest of the drinks. When I place the last one in front of Cam I see him grab the beer and tilt the bottle to his lips.

Within seconds what fills his mouth spews right back out. "What the fuck?" he sputters, wiping his lips with the back of his hand.

"Is there a problem with your beer, Jase?" I ask, nothing but sweet innocence coating my tone.

His furious eyes snap to mine. "What the hell did you put in here?"

"Just the Tabasco you ordered. That was you, wasn't it?" I ask, tapping my bottom lip. "Or maybe it was someone else…"

Laughter erupts around the table; Cam's being the loudest of all. "This is the best fucking thing I've ever seen."

Jake gives me a nod of approval while Austin reaches over the table, giving me his fist. "There's that Evans's spirit."

Feeling proud of myself, I tap knuckles with him. Jase, however, looks less than amused. He looks downright pissed.

With more courage than I feel, I saunter over to him, placing my hands on either side of his chair. Leaning in close, I try to ignore the way his alluring masculine scent invades my senses. "I tell you what, Crawford. If your mouth is a little hot why don't you head up to the bar and *fetch* yourself some water."

Something dark flashes in his eyes before his gaze drops to my mouth. A gasp parts my lips when he hooks a hand behind my neck and pulls me in closer. So close that I can feel his warm breath whisper across my lips.

"You just waged a war, little girl. I hope you're prepared."

Swallowing past my dry throat, I try to calm my wild heartbeat, refusing to let him rattle me. "No, Jase, I just ended it." I give his freshly shaven jaw a gentle slap. "Now, let me go get you another beer…minus the hot sauce."

I grace him with the same wink he gave me earlier then move out from under his hand and walk away. My steps are slow and faked with confidence as I make my way back over to the bar. The air that's been trapped inside of my lungs finally releases once I reach the counter.

"Jesus murphy. What the hell was that?" Zoey asks, fanning herself. "I thought you were going to slip him the tongue."

"So did I," I admit on a heavy breath.

Seconds pass before we burst into a fit of laughter.

"God, Zoey." My hand moves to the back of my neck where I still burn from his touch. I swear the guy is some sort of magician to have that kind of effect on women.

"I told you he was hot."

"Yeah, he's hot. And arrogant and infuriating and—"

She raises her hand with a chuckle. "I get the point."

Shaking my head, I try to erase the last five minutes from my mind…and body. "Get me another bottle of Bud, please. I'll pay for it before I leave tonight."

She quirks a brow at me but does as I ask, popping the cap.

"Thanks." Swiping the bottle, I start back to their table. My steps falter when I see a few girls have joined them, one being Stephanie Taylor. The town bicycle and Jase's ex. She sidles up next to him, wrapping her arms around one of his biceps. He doesn't reciprocate but he doesn't push her away either.

A sick feeling forms in the pit of my stomach. A feeling that should have no bearing on me whatsoever because Jase is no one to me. I can't stand him.

So why the hell do I care?

Because I don't like Stephanie. It's her fault Sawyer and Jase hate each other. She made Sawyer think she and Jase had broken up when he slept with her. However, I must admit that Sawyer was stupid to mess with her in the first place. Everyone knows that girl is nothing but trouble.

Arriving at their table, I avoid eye contact and place the new beer down in front of Jase before picking up the old one. My plan is to keep moving—until the bitch speaks.

"When did you start working here?" she asks in a patronizing tone. "I thought you are a babysitter."

I'm a preschool teacher and she knows it, but I don't bother correcting her. Instead, I turn back around and ignore the way she clings to Jase. "My friend needs extra help tonight to make sure whores like you aren't spreading their diseases."

Muffled chuckles sound around the table.

Her eyes narrow in hatred. "Go back to the playground you're always at and leave places like this for real women."

"I'd pick those children over the likes of you any day. Their IQ is much higher and so is their class." I start away, refusing to waste any more time on her, but what she says next has me freezing in place.

"How's your family, Samantha? Oh wait, that's right, they all left because they couldn't stand you."

I fight like hell against the pain that infiltrates my chest. She's wrong. She doesn't know what she's talking about. Logically, I know this, but it doesn't stop it from hurting. She knew exactly where to hit.

"Shut the fuck up, Stephanie."

Surprisingly, the harsh words come from Jase. A few of the other guys start in on her too, but I don't stick around to hear it. I continue on, not wanting her to see how much her words hurt.

For the next hour, I avoid their table like the plague and hand it off to Tara. I can't trust myself to be near that bitch. I'm not usually a violent person but for her I'd make an exception.

Spotting a few empty tables in the back that need clearing, I grab the bottle of cleaner and my dishtowel then head that way. As I'm wiping one down I sense eyes burning into my back. Looking over my shoulder, I find Jase watching me. There's something in his gaze as he stares at me, something I've never seen from him before. I can't pinpoint what it is but it's captivating, like an invisible magnet pulling me in. I'm so caught up in it that I don't realize I'm not alone until it's too late.

"Hello, Samantha."

Every muscle in my body stiffens; dread twisting my stomach at the regal voice. Straightening, I turn to find Grant. The last person on earth I want to see. I'd even take bicycle bitch over him.

He takes me in from head to toe, his nose wrinkling in distaste. Not surprising. My long, wavy hair, jean skirt, and black tank top would never be up to his standards. Good thing I don't give a shit about his standards anymore.

Of course, he is in immaculate condition. He's dressed in his usual business attire with not one strand of his light brown hair out of place.

Obviously, another *late night* at the office.

Crossing my arms over my chest, I take a step back from him, feeling my back meet the wall, and quickly realize I'm cornered. Definitely not something I want when dealing with him.

"What are you doing here?" I ask, skipping over any pleasantries.

"I came to see you. I had no choice since you've been refusing my calls." His voice is calm but there's no denying the anger in his crystal blue eyes. An anger that used to scare the hell out of me and still does, if I'm being honest, but I'd never let him know it.

I will never give him that power over me again.

"We have nothing more to say to each other."

"Yes, we do. Now this needs to stop, Samantha. You're acting like a foolish adolescent."

My teeth grind at the way he uses my full name, scolding me like a child.

"It's time to get over your tantrum and—"

"This is not a tantrum," I snap. "We're over, Grant."

"The hell we are!" Fear grips my chest as he steps closer to me, his eyes flashing in fury.

Stay calm, Sam. He won't touch you. Not here.

Not ever again.

"Everything all right?"

My head snaps to the side, unexpected relief swamping me at the sight of Jase.

"Fine," Grant answers before I can, his tone icy. "We're having a conversation, if you don't mind."

"Actually, we're done." I seize the opportunity to slide out from the corner I'm in and move closer to Jase. "Grant was just leaving."

At the feel of his furious gaze on me, my eyes drop to the floor, silence hanging heavily in the air.

"Very well," Grant says, sounding a lot calmer than I know he is.

"We'll talk about this another time, Samantha."

I shake my head but it's pointless since he's already turned his back and walked away. A shaky breath escapes me, my hand resting on my queasy stomach.

I should have known he would show up sooner or later.

I clue in to the person standing next to me, feeling his eyes boring holes into the side of my head.

"You want to tell me what that was all about?"

"It's nothing," I mumble, my throat burning with humiliation that it had to be him who showed up at the right time.

"Really? That's why you're shaking right now?"

I look down at my trembling hands, angry with myself for letting Grant rattle me so much. Gripping the washcloth tighter, I move to walk past him, but he doesn't let me.

His fingers wrap around my arm in a gentle grip. "Sam…"

"Just let it go, Jase." Pulling my arm free, I walk away and head into the back for some privacy. It takes me a few minutes before I'm able to find my composure again. When I return to finish my shift, I try not to think about Grant, but it proves impossible. So many emotions storming inside of me, especially regret.

Once the place dies down, Zoey offers for me to go home. I take it because I'm not being much use right now anyway. My head is not in it anymore and I think she senses that. It's obvious she never saw Grant come in; otherwise, she would've had a field day with his ass.

After giving her a hug, I grab my jacket and purse then pay for Jase's beer that I sabotaged. Before leaving, I glance over at their table one last time but don't see him there. My first thought is he left with Stephanie, but I spot her by the far corner near the bathroom. I give the rest of the guys a wave good-bye then head out into the dark night.

As I round the corner of the building where my car is parked, I come to a hard stop when I see Grant standing there, waiting for me.

Acknowledgements

I'm blessed to have so many amazing people who love and support me in this beautiful journey I'm on. Most of them have been with me from the very beginning. They've had my back, believed in me, and wouldn't let me give up when times were daunting.

To everyone who has been a part of this amazing journey with me—family, my beautiful editor, betas, friends, my author groups, bloggers, and readers around the world. You know who you are. Thank you. I love and cherish every single one of you.

A special shout-out to the brave men of Fire Station Two and Captain Gyepesi aka Captain Gypsi, who so graciously allowed me to be a part of the family for a night. I found you funny and admirable. I knew the moment I met you, I would make you the captain in this series.

Thank you to the rest of you for the courageous, honorable work you do and for welcoming me into your station. An extended thanks to Kevin Royle for continuing to answer any questions I have and extending an open invitation to the station. I appreciate it more than you know.

You men are true heroes.

Author Bio

K.C. Lynn is a small town girl who was born and raised in Western Canada. She grew up in a family of four children—two sisters and a brother. Her mother was the lady who baked homemade goods for everyone on the street and her father was a respected man who worked in the RCMP. He's since retired and now works for the criminal justice system. This being one of the things that inspires K.C. to write about the trials and triumphs of our heroes.

K.C. married her high school sweetheart and they started a big family of their own—two adorable girls and a set of handsome twin boys. As much as they loved their hometown, it was time for new beginnings so they picked up and moved to the South where everyone says 'y'all' and eats biscuits and gravy for breakfast.

It was her love for romance books that gave K.C. the courage to sit down and write her own novel. It was then a beautiful world opened up and she found what she was meant to do…write.

When K.C.'s not spending time with her family she can be found in her writing cave, living in the fabulous minds of her characters and their stories.

Made in the USA
San Bernardino, CA
20 August 2018